## A GRISLY DISCOVERY

By now we were under the bridge, and Otis's voice echoed off the stone wall. He was down in the water, standing kind of stiff and funny, barking at something.

"What's wrong?" Parker waded into the creek and grabbed Otis's collar.

"Just pray it's not another skunk," I yelled from the bank.

Parker glanced at me. His face was pale and he was tugging hard at Otis. "It's no skunk," he whispered, stumbling backward in his haste to get out of the water.

"Well, what is it?" I peered over Parker's shoulder. At first all I saw was a bundle of rags, old clothes or something caught in the roots by the bank. Then I saw a shoe. And a hand sort of waving at me under the water. But the worst part was the face. It looked like a rock, white and bumpy, hair streaming away like weeds, mouth and eyes open, staring right at me.

I think I screamed when I realized what it was.

Other novels by
# MARY DOWNING HAHN

Closed for the Season
All the Lovely Bad Ones
Deep and Dark and Dangerous
Witch Catcher
The Old Willis Place
Hear the Wind Blow
Anna on the Farm
Promises to the Dead
Anna All Year Round
As Ever, Gordy
The Gentleman Outlaw and Me—Eli
Look for Me by Moonlight
Time for Andrew
The Wind Blows Backward
Stepping on the Cracks
The Doll in the Garden
Tallahassee Higgins
Wait Till Helen Comes
Daphne's Book

# THE DEAD MAN IN INDIAN CREEK

## MARY DOWNING HAHN

𝆕 sandpiper

Houghton Mifflin Harcourt
Boston   New York

www.sandpiperbooks.com

The Library of Congress has cataloged the hardcover edition as follows:

Hahn, Mary Downing.
The dead man in Indian Creek / Mary Downing Hahn.
p. cm.
Summary: When Matt and Parker learn the body they found in Indian Creek is a
drug-related death, they fear Parker's mother may be involved.

[1. Mystery and detective stories.] I. Title.
PZ7.H1256Dd 1989
[Fic]—dc20

ISBN: 978-0-395-52397-1
ISBN: 978-0-547-24880-6 pb

Manufactured in the United States of America
DOM 10 9 8 7 6 5 4

4500276518

For my nieces,
Anne Downing and Livia Collins

# DEAD MAN IN INDIAN CREEK

# ·1·

IF PARKER PETTENGILL hadn't wanted to go camping, we never would have found the dead man in Indian Creek, and, believe me, we would have been a whole lot better off. But isn't that the way it always is? You look back on some little decision you made and realize all the things that happened because of it, and you think to yourself "if only I'd known," but, of course, you couldn't have known.

Anyway, there Parker and I were, sitting on my back porch one Saturday afternoon, enjoying the sunshine as we watched the leaves slowly fall through the quiet October air. It was Indian summer, and the day was so warm and lazy I could have sat there forever.

But not Parker. Lately he'd been edgy and restless, always wanting to go somewhere, meet somebody, do something. If we stayed in the same place for more than five minutes, he'd start drumming his fingers on tabletops or tapping his foot or biting his fingernails.

Nervous energy, my mother called it, but he wore me out.

"Hey, you know what we should do?" he said.

"Nothing," I said, and I meant it. I was perfectly content just feeling the sun warm my back and smelling something that might be brownies baking in the oven.

"No, seriously, Armentrout." Parker poked me in the arm, just hard enough to hurt. Since we started junior high school, he's been calling me by my last name; I guess he thinks it sounds cool and sophisticated, but it kind of gives me a pain. I mean I've been answering to Matt or Matthew all my life, but now all of a sudden it's Armentrout this and Armentrout that, and it takes getting used to.

"Let's camp out tonight," Parker went on. "This might be the last good weekend."

His straight blond hair was hanging in his eyes, his bony knees were poking out of the holes in his jeans, and he had the eager look on his face he always gets when he's excited about something. I often see the same expression on his dog Otis's face when he's begging for a walk.

"Where do you want to go?" I asked, unable to infuse the slightest bit of enthusiasm into my voice.

"How about Indian Creek? It's still warm enough for swimming, and we could fish in the morning. We might even see that blue heron again." He gave me another little punch. "Come on, what do you say?"

Well, I wasn't really in the mood to pack up my camping gear and ride my bike eight miles out of town and who knows how far down the creek. But no matter what I said, Parker kept insisting, and finally I gave in. He was, as my parents often pointed out, a natural-born leader, and I was a natural-born follower.

I went into the house to tell my mother about Parker's and my plans, but she was too busy making a bunch of little bread-dough Christmas tree ornaments to pay me much attention. She only had a couple of weeks to get ready for the Woodcroft Fall Festival, and she was counting on her sales to bring in extra money for Christmas shopping.

What I'd thought were brownies baking in the oven were more ornaments, so I took a handful of cookies out of a box and poured glasses of milk for Parker and me. After a while, I cleared my throat and said, "Mom, Parker and I are camping out at Indian Creek. Okay?"

She looked up from the bread dough and frowned. "Overnight, Matthew?"

I knew what Mom was thinking. She always worries I'll get into trouble under Parker's influence. According to her, his mother, Pam, doesn't keep a close enough eye on him. It's true that Parker spends a lot of time alone, but it isn't his mother's fault. His father was killed in a car crash when Parker was a baby, and she has to work. So what if she goes out at night and leaves Parker home by himself once in a while? No matter what Mom thinks, Parker doesn't take advantage of it.

"We want to go one more time," I said, "while it's still so nice and warm and all." I munched a cookie and waited for Mom to answer. I was kind of hoping she'd say no and save me all the trouble of getting the tent, an old K-mart special, out of the attic.

But you know how parents are—if I'd been dying to go, she would have said no, but since I wasn't all that hot on it, she said yes.

Then she had to add, "The exercise would do you good."

That made Parker laugh. For some reason, he and I are developing at very different rates. A year or two ago, we were about the same size, but now that we're twelve, Parker is getting taller and leaner every day, and I seem to be staying the same height but getting rounder. I've even developed this awful little spare tire around my waist like a middle-aged man, and I sure didn't appreciate Mom's drawing Parker's attention to it.

Leaving Parker with Mom, I got the tent out of the attic. Then I threw some stuff in my backpack. On my way to the kitchen, I had the bad luck to pass my little sister Charity in the hall. If ever a kid was misnamed, Charity was. At the sight of me, she and her friend Tiffany started cackling like chickens in a barn.

"Fatty, fatty two by four," they chanted. "Can't get through the kitchen door!"

I paused and glared down at her. Should I care what a couple of six-year-old twits said? "Stupid," I muttered.

Charity stuck out her tongue and made her bratty little face even uglier, but I ignored her. Pushing her out of my way, I stuck my head into the kitchen.

"Come on, Parker," I said. "Let's get out of here."

He smiled at Mom, took one more cookie, and followed me down the back steps. No matter how Mom feels about Pam, Parker always manages to charm her into liking him.

We strapped the tent on my bike and rode over to Parker's house. He lives on the other side of town, not a long ride, and we pedaled slowly, enjoying the weather. All around us leaves drifted down, yellow and red and gold. In the big yards on Appleton Street, people were raking them up as fast as they fell, and the air was mellow with wood smoke.

The houses we passed were the biggest and oldest in town, and almost all of them were decorated for Halloween. Jack-o'-lanterns grinned on front porches, scarecrows lounged on the steps, ghosts made of bedsheets hung in the upper windows of a house with a tower on the side.

Like a little kid, I was looking forward to Halloween and the Fall Festival—two whole days of food and fun, costumes and prizes, parades and speeches. It was the most exciting thing Woodcroft ever did, and people came every year from as far away as Washington, D.C., to buy handmade crafts and food, watch the parade, have their faces painted, and ride in horse-drawn hay wagons.

Everybody wore costumes, and there were prizes for things like the funniest or the scariest or the prettiest. Last year my parents won the best couple prize for dressing up like Bonnie and Clyde and shooting everybody with water pistols. It was very embarrassing, and I was glad they were dressing as George and Martha Washington this year.

"What are you going to be for Halloween?" I asked Parker as we bumped over the train tracks and coasted down Cat Tail Hill.

Parker glanced at me. His hair was blowing straight back from his face, and he had his hands in the back pockets of his jeans, showing off his perfect balance and nerve. He shrugged. "Some kind of monster," he said. "Frankenstein maybe, or one of the Walking Dead."

"I was thinking of Dracula," I told him. "Mom has a long black cape, and Dad's got an old waiter's uniform he wore years ago."

Parker nodded. "I saw some great makeup kits in the Ben Franklin Store. You can get fangs and green glop for your face and this stuff that makes really gross scars."

We talked about Halloween the rest of the way to Parker's, planning the route we'd take for trick or treating and speculating about which houses to hit first. We didn't want to make the mistake we'd made last year when we'd found out Miss Atkins was handing out full-size candy bars. By the time we got to her house, she'd given them all away, and Parker and I ended up with a couple of pennies instead of a big chocolate bar. This year, we told ourselves, Miss Atkins would be number one on our list.

But, of course, at that moment, racing around a curve at the bottom of the hill, we didn't know about the dead man and the effect he was going to have on our Halloween.

T PARKER'S HOUSE, we dumped our bikes in the driveway. His mother was on the front porch, and my heart went flippety-flip at the sight of her.

Wearing faded jeans and an old, paint-splattered T-shirt, she was sanding an oak icebox, something she'd brought home from the Olde Mill Antique Shoppe where she works. Her long blond hair hung around her face in curly waves, and a band of freckles bridged her nose, making her look more like Parker's sister than his mother. I know it sounds dumb, but sometimes I think I'm in love with her even though she's almost thirty-two years old.

"Hey, Park, Matt—how are my favorite guys?" She asked.

"We're going camping, Pam," Parker said. "Out at Indian Creek. Okay?"

When I first met Parker, it surprised me to hear him

call his mother Pam, but, even though I still couldn't imagine calling my mother Cathy, I was used to it by now. Besides, Pam suited her better than Mom or Mother.

"Sounds like fun." Pam went back to work on the icebox. "If I were twelve, I'd go with you."

"You can come," I said, hoping she was hinting for an invitation.

Pam shook her head and laughed. "No, Matt. You don't want old folks spoiling your fun."

"You're not old!" I paused to admire the icebox, but Parker gave me a poke in the side, ruining my attempt to look cool and mature.

"Let's get going," he said. "You move so slow, it'll be dark before we get there."

Reluctantly I left Pam on the porch and followed Parker to his room. Unlike my house, Parker's place is real small. A shot-gun house, my dad says, because you could open the front door, fire a gun, and the bullet would go straight out the back door.

"Hey." I paused in front of a huge color television set in the living room. "When did you get this?"

Parker stopped in the kitchen doorway and gave me a funny look, sort of mad and embarrassed at the same time. "Evans brought it over here," he muttered.

"Pam's boss?" I whistled and ran one hand over the smooth finish on the cabinet. "How come he loaned it to you?"

Parker didn't answer. He just shrugged, flipped his

hair out of his eyes, and walked into the kitchen.

"It must be nice having a boss that generous," I said. "I bet Mr. Stemmer wouldn't even loan my dad a pocket calculator."

Since Parker was still ignoring me, I stopped to examine a heap of shabby antique dolls on the kitchen table. Pam had already fixed a few of them, but most of the poor things were lying around in pieces. Bald, eyeless heads, china hands, bodies, wigs, piles of little dresses and shoes littered the table.

"Better call the Red Cross," I told Parker. "These folks need help."

I picked up one of the victims. The dark brows painted right above her eyes gave her face a criminal look reminding me of old photographs of outlaws, sort of ruthless and stupid. "Did you ever see that TV show about the killer doll?" I called to Parker.

But he was too busy pulling camping gear out from under his bed to be interested in what I was saying. Dumping a sweatshirt and some other things into his backpack, he returned to the kitchen and grabbed a couple of cans of Dinty Moore Stew, half a loaf of bread, and some brown bananas. "You got any cash?" he asked.

I checked my pockets. "Three dollars," I said, glad I hadn't spent all my lawn-raking money. "And some change."

Parker nodded. "We'll stop at Seven-Eleven and buy sodas and Twinkies for breakfast."

Picking up his sleeping bag, Parker followed me out

onto the porch. We were just in time to see George Evans getting out of his MG.

"What's he want?" Parker slammed his gear down and watched Evans saunter up the sidewalk.

From the porch, I could see the top of Evans's head as he climbed the steps toward us. His hair was getting a little thin on top, even though he arranged what was left very carefully. He also had a spare tire which you couldn't dismiss as baby fat, not at his age. He was at least forty, maybe more, but he dressed like some preppy-type just out of college—pink polo shirt, khaki pants, loafers. My mom told me once she thought he was one good-looking guy, but I sure couldn't see anything handsome about him.

"Listen," Parker whispered, "if he's sticking around here, we're camping in the backyard, okay? I'm not leaving Pam alone with him."

I swallowed hard and stared at Parker. Surely he wasn't implying that Pam enjoyed Evans's company. She was much too beautiful to waste her time with a man like him.

"Hi, everybody." Evans embraced us all with the grin he used on the ladies who flocked to his antique shop. Maybe it charmed them, maybe it even charmed Pam and my mother, but it sure didn't charm Parker and me.

"How does it look, George?" Pam gestured at the icebox.

"Beautiful." Evans ran his fingers lightly over the smooth wood. "This is really fine." The way he smiled at Pam, you'd think it was her skin he was touching, not the icebox.

As Evans bent to inspect the brass fittings on the icebox door, Otis came charging around the corner of the house. Even though he was a German Shepherd, a breed not known for its friendliness, Otis was gentle with everyone but Evans. Whenever he saw him, he went into a frenzy.

Parker claimed it all started when Evans was showing him some wrestling holds. "Otis might not be real smart," Parker said, "but he'd kill anyone who tried to hurt me."

At any rate, Otis moved so fast he actually had his teeth in Evans's rear end before the man knew what was happening.

"Get him off! Get him off!" Evans yelled as Parker grabbed Otis's collar and dragged the dog away, still snarling.

Evans rattled off a couple of fine words while Pam inspected the damage.

"He didn't break the skin, George," she said, "but he did make a teeny tiny rip in your pants."

I couldn't decide if she were fighting back laughter or tears, but I was hoping for the former. After all, Evans had a big rear end and he couldn't have been in a better position for Otis to bite it.

"Teeny tiny rip?" Evans craned his neck around and almost threw his hip out of joint trying to see the seat of his pants. "I paid seventy-five dollars for this pair of slacks!"

"I think I can mend them," Pam said. Then she added, "I'm so sorry, George."

"You ought to get rid of that animal." Evans glared at Otis who growled back and struggled to get away from Parker. "He's a nuisance. And a liability. Suppose he bites the mailman? Or the newspaper boy? You could get sued for everything you own."

"Which wouldn't be much," Pam said.

"You're the only person he ever tries to bite," Parker muttered, but Evans pretended not to hear him.

Turning to Pam, he split his face into another grin and said, "Well, are we still on for dinner tonight, beautiful?"

She smiled and nodded. "You'll have to give me half an hour to get ready," she said. "I wasn't expecting you so soon."

Then Pam looked at us. "Parker and Matt are going camping tonight," she said.

"Nice weather for it," Evans observed.

Parker studied Evans's face for a second. Then he squinted at the cloudless sky. "I think it's starting to look like rain," he said. "Maybe we should pitch the tent in the backyard. Don't you agree, Armentrout?"

"You're right," I said as Parker nudged me. "We better stay here."

Tipping his head back, Evans slipped his hands in his pockets and jingled his keys. "It's not going to rain," he said. "Sky's as clear as a bell."

"I said you could go, Parker," Pam said.

Parker glanced at Evans and frowned. "I'll leave

Otis with you then," he said to Pam. "You might need some protection."

"Oh, no," Pam said firmly. "He's your dog, Parker, and your responsibility. Take him with you."

Otis grinned up at Parker and thumped his tail, but I was sure our trip was ruined. Taking Otis somewhere is almost as bad as dragging Charity along. You spend half your time calling him or chasing after him. The last time he went camping with us, he smelled a skunk in the middle of the night, knocked the tent down trying to get at him, and then, of course, almost asphyxiated us when we got him back. I never smelled anything like it—he must have met the king of the skunks. It took five dollars' worth of tomato juice shampoos just to get the odor down to a point where you could stand to be within three feet of him.

Of course, Evans agreed with Pam. "Don't worry about your mom," he said to Parker, "I'll keep her company." He slid his arm around Pam's waist and gave her a hug. To my disappointment, Pam snuggled closer instead of pulling away from him.

"Go on, boys," she said. "Soon the weather will be too cold for camping. You might as well enjoy it while it lasts."

Well, we didn't really have much choice, did we? Glumly we loaded our bikes and pedaled away, leaving Pam and Evans waving to us from the porch. They were happy, Otis was happy, but Parker was glaring at me as if the camping trip had been all my idea.

# ·3·

B Y THE TIME we got to our camping site, I was totally exhausted. After all, it isn't every day I ride my bike for eight miles loaded down with a tent and a sleeping bag and a knapsack full of clothes and food.

But do you think Parker was tired? Not a bit. Right away he unrolled the tent and made me help set it up.

"What's the matter, Armentrout?" He sat back on his heels. "Are you out of shape or something? Or is it just too many Twinkies?"

Frankly I was getting tired of being kidded about my weight. It wasn't like I was really fat. So I didn't look at him, didn't even answer him. If I said anything, I was going to get mad, I just knew it, and then Parker would get mad and we'd have a big fight and end up having a horrible time. I got out my Swiss Army Knife and started whittling at a twig and whistling, pretending I hadn't heard a word he'd spoken.

"Making a stick for marshmallows?" Parker wanted to know.

Forgetting my resolve, I looked at him. "What's the matter with you?" Angrily, I broke the stick I'd been whittling and tossed it into the bushes. If we were going to have a fight, okay, I was ready. Let him sock me, I'd sock him back, and then I'd sit on him, my ultimate advantage, right?

But Parker just stood up and brushed the dirt from the knees of his jeans. Then he sighed and jammed his hands in his back pockets. "I'm sorry," he mumbled. "It's not you, Armentrout, it's George Evans. I hate that creep!"

Without looking at me, he walked off and started skipping stones across the creek. I watched him for a while. Parker had so much skill he could make a stone dance all the way across the water to the other side.

"What's Evans done?" I asked. "Has it got something to do with Pam or what?"

Parker threw a stone so viciously it ripped into the water like a bullet. "Pam's in love with him," he muttered.

In the sudden silence, I could hear a woodpecker drumming away in the woods across the creek. "You're crazy," I said. "Pam wouldn't fall for somebody like Evans. Not in a million years."

Parker looked at me. His face was red, and his eyes shone like they had tears in them. "Last night she worked real late, and he brought her home. I looked out my window and saw him kissing her." He picked up another stone and hurled it into the water. It didn't skip once.

"She was letting him?" My heart beat harder, and I caught myself clutching my chest like a girl. "She wasn't fighting him off or anything?"

"You saw him hug her before we left. Was she putting up any fuss about it?" Parker turned his head, hiding his face. "She couldn't wait to get rid of us today."

I started to say something, but Parker was already walking away from me. "Forget it," he muttered. "I don't want to talk about it, okay?"

*

For the rest of the afternoon, Parker and I fooled around. We tried fishing, went for a swim, climbed a few trees, but the only one having any real fun was Otis. He ran into the river and out again, shaking himself all over Parker and me. Then he tore off into the woods, barking and carrying on. I never saw such a happy dog. But he couldn't get Parker out of his black mood and neither could I.

After dark, we sat around our fire eating canned stew and Twinkies, but we didn't talk much. By then, even Otis was feeling kind of done in, so it was a relief to get undressed and crawl into our sleeping bags.

Just as I was about to doze off, Parker said, "Let's get up early. I brought my binoculars and I want to look for some birds. Maybe that heron's still around."

"Yeah." I squirmed deeper into my sleeping bag, trying to get away from the tree root poking my backside. Birds. The last thing I wanted to do was go looking for birds at dawn.

Parker was silent for a while, and I snuggled deeper into my sleeping bag. Then he said, "Are you awake, Armentrout?"

Actually I'd been right on the edge of a dream, but I opened my eyes and turned my head toward his side of the tent. Otis was curled up between us, twitching every now and then, so I couldn't see Parker. "Yes," I said, "I'm awake."

"What if Pam marries Evans?" Parker asked.

"She's got better taste than that," I said. "He's a jerk."

"Why does she let him kiss her then?" Parker asked. "And why does she spend so much time with him? And how come we have a huge TV and a VCR and a microwave, not to mention the brand-new clothes Pam's wearing all of a sudden?"

I stared at Parker, trying to see the expression on his face, but it was too dark in the tent to make out more than the shaggy outline of his head.

While I was trying to think of a good explanation for Evans's generosity, Parker said, "She talks about him all the time, how smart he is, how rich he is, how good-looking he is." He paused. "Yesterday I caught her looking at travel brochures—cruises to the Bahamas, tours to Disney World, all kinds of stuff. When she saw me, she shoved them under a pile of bills and said they were just junk mail."

"Maybe they were," I said. "Mom's always getting letters that make it sound like you've won a trip to Hawaii or Australia. Then you read the fine print and find out you have to subscribe to magazines or something to be eligible."

"Not these," Parker said. "I looked at them later when she wasn't home. They came from a travel agent in Baltimore, and they were addressed to Evans. I think they're planning their honeymoon."

"You're nuts," I said.

"You don't live with her, Armentrout. You don't see her every day like I do." The bitter edge in Parker's voice cut through the darkness. "She doesn't care what happens to me anymore."

"Come on, Parker," I muttered, "you know that's not true." I wanted to say something nice, something comforting, but I didn't know how or what. "She's had other boyfriends," I tried. "Remember good old Jerome? She didn't marry him and run off to the Bahamas, did she?"

"You're a lot of help." Parker rolled over in his sleeping bag and didn't say anything else. Then, except for this horrible snoring sound Otis was making, the tent got real quiet.

I finally fell asleep, but I kept waking up all night long, shifting from one side to the other. The ground was hard, I was cold and uncomfortable, and Otis was curled up right next to me, smelling like the creek and breathing in my face. Add to that an owl screeching and Parker muttering in his sleep. Why do I always forget how much I hate camping?

*

It seemed to me I'd just closed my eyes when Parker woke me up. The tent was dim in the gray morning light, and the trees outside were all shrouded in mist. I could hear Otis running around in the bushes, sniffing at things. It would take more than a little fog to slow him down.

"Come on, Armentrout." Parker held a Twinkie a few inches from my nose. "Breakfast time."

I ate the Twinkie and then pulled my clothes on fast, hoping to get warm. Reluctantly, I followed Parker down the path along the creek. He had his binoculars around his neck, looking everywhere for the heron, though how he'd see him in all the mist I didn't know.

After trudging along for about fifteen minutes, we rounded a bend in the creek. Up ahead was an old stone bridge arching high over the water. Suddenly Parker motioned me to stop and be quiet. At first I thought he'd finally spotted the heron, but then I realized there was a person on the bridge.

Almost soundlessly, Parker backed up and I did too. But not Otis. With his usual stupidity, he charged around me and started barking. Dropping his binoculars, Parker grabbed the dog and yanked him backward into the bushes. "Hush!" he hissed at Otis, startling the animal into silence.

"Keep him quiet," Parker whispered to me as he raised his binoculars again.

"Who is it?" No matter how hard I strained my eyes, I couldn't recognize the man. All I could tell was that he'd heard the dog and was looking around, trying to see where the barking had come from.

Otis whimpered and squirmed, but I kept him still while Parker watched the man walk over the bridge and disappear into the bushes. Was he coming this way? No. A car started, and I listened to it drive away.

"Who was it?" I asked Parker again.

Parker stared at me. "Evans," he said. "Didn't you recognize the sound of his MG?"

"What was he doing here at this time of morning?" I scratched my head. Quite frankly, Evans didn't seem like the type who'd be up and out this early. I couldn't imagine him fishing, birdwatching, or even jogging, certainly not eight miles out of town on Fulton Farm Road on a Sunday morning.

"I don't know," Parker said as Otis, free of my grip, ran off, nose to the ground, tail wagging.

Parker started walking again, his binoculars swinging on the end of their strap, and I trudged after him. The damp grass was soaking through my shoes, I was stiff from sleeping on the hard ground, and I was still hungry. Worst of all, it looked like Parker was slumping back into the mood he'd been in yesterday, and I was sorry we'd seen Evans. He seemed to be ruining everything for Parker and me.

Just then we heard Otis barking again. "Now what's gotten into that dog?" Parker walked a little faster, and I had to really push myself to keep up with him. Even so, he got to Otis before I did.

By now we were under the bridge, and Otis's voice echoed off the stone walls. He was down in the water, standing kind of stiff and funny, barking at something.

"What's wrong?" Parker waded into the creek and grabbed Otis's collar.

"Just pray it's not another skunk," I yelled from the bank.

Parker glanced at me. His face was pale and he was tugging hard at Otis. "It's no skunk," he whispered, stumbling backward in his haste to get out of the water.

"Well, what is it?" I peered over Parker's shoulder. At first all I saw was a bundle of rags, old clothes or something caught in the roots by the bank. Then I saw a shoe. And a hand sort of waving at me under the water. But the worst part was the face. It looked like a rock, white and bumpy, hair streaming away like weeds, mouth and eyes open, staring right at me.

I think I screamed when I realized what it was. Then Parker and I were dragging Otis away from the dead man, slipping and stumbling as we tried to get out of the creek and up the hill to Fulton Farm Road.

# ·4·

BY THE TIME we reached the road, I was too out of breath to say anything, but it didn't matter because Parker and Otis kept on going like they were planning to run all the way to town. I tried to keep up with them, but after a while I gasped out, "Wait, Parker, wait."

He slowed down and looked back at me. Then he sighed and stood still while I huffed and puffed toward him. My side ached and my legs felt like noodles and I wanted to fling myself down in the weeds and lie there for the rest of the day. But I knew if I closed my eyes I'd see that face looking up at me from under the water.

"What are we going to do?" I asked.

"Tell the police," Parker said. "That guy was *murdered,* I saw the bullet hole in his forehead." He glanced over his shoulder, but the road was empty behind us.

"Murdered?" Every single hair on my whole body shot straight up. If Parker was right, the killer might still be here, hiding in the woods on either side of the road, watching us, pointing his gun, his finger about to squeeze the trigger.

The same thought must have occurred to Parker because he started running, and so did Otis and I.

"Have you ever seen a dead man before?" Parker asked when we slowed down again to rest.

"Just my grandfather," I said, "but he was in a coffin at Grant's Funeral Home with flowers all around him and his eyes closed. You know, just lying there like he was asleep or something." I saw that face under the water with its eyes open and its hair streaming out, and I felt a little sick, like maybe I shouldn't have eaten those Twinkies.

"That's different, though. Seeing a person laid out all formal." Parker shook his head. "This guy looked like something in a movie, didn't he?"

I nodded, thinking of all the dead people I'd seen in movies. "He looked lots worse," I said.

"There was something familiar about him," Parker mused as we jogged along. "I know him from somewhere, I'm sure of it."

"Not me," I said. I was certain the dead man and his killer were strangers passing through, people who'd turned off the Interstate and had nothing to do with my town or me. After all, when was the last time anybody had been murdered in Woodcroft? It wasn't the kind of place where people killed each other. No, whoever the killer was, he'd be a million miles away by now and no danger to me.

"What do you think Evans was doing on the bridge?" Parker asked.

I'd forgotten all about Evans. "What do you mean?"

"Maybe he dumped that guy in the creek."

"You think George Evans killed him?" As much as I was beginning to dislike him, I couldn't imagine Evans murdering somebody. He wasn't the violent type.

"Maybe," Parker said. "You can bet he wasn't on the bridge just to see the sunrise."

"But why would he do it?"

Parker shrugged. By now we were at the edge of town, right at the top of the hill in front of the old Watkins house. Looking down Fulton Farm Road from here, you could see both the Methodist and the Baptist churches and most of Main Street, including the police station and the Olde Mill Antique Shoppe right on the corner of Windsor Road. The town had that early Sunday morning stillness. Too early for church, no stores open, nobody about.

"Are you telling the police we saw Evans?" I asked Parker.

He nodded and called Otis back from the cat he'd spotted on the Watkins' porch. Sprinting ahead of me, Parker and Otis tore down Fulton Farm Road toward the police station. By then I was so tired and my stomach felt so upset from running I didn't care whether he got there first or not. In some ways, I would have liked to go home and leave everything to Parker. Let him talk to the police, let him be interviewed, let him be the hero. I was sick of the whole thing.

*

When I caught up with Parker at the police station, though, he was standing on the steps waiting for me. He looked almost as nervous as I felt.

"What are we going to do with Otis?" I asked Parker, stalling for time. "We can't take him inside and we don't have his leash." I shifted my weight back and forth from one foot to the other and watched Otis sniffing a parking meter.

Parker grabbed Otis by the collar and dragged him through the door. "When they hear what we have to tell them," he said, "they won't make a fuss about a dog."

So even though the sign on the door said, "No Pets," Otis began making himself at home, sniffing and scratching his fleas. The policeman on desk duty was Sergeant Williams, the one who came to school every fall and talked to us about drugs and bicycle safety and stuff like that.

"Can't you kids read?" He put down a Styrofoam coffee cup and scowled at Otis. "Get that dog out of here."

"There's a dead man in Indian Creek," Parker said. His voice came out squeaky and high. "We saw him while we were camping."

"Is this some kind of joke?" Sergeant Williams stood up. His belly hung over his gun belt and he needed a shave. He didn't look nearly as friendly as he did at school.

"Me and my friend were hiking up the creek when we saw him. He's under the bridge on Fulton Farm Road." Parker met Williams's frown head-on, not giving an inch.

The policeman's head swiveled toward me. "You saw the body too?"

I nodded, too scared to say anything. The face was back again, staring at me from its dead eyes, its mouth open, its hair swirling, its hand waving. I could feel my stomach churning and I forced myself to swallow hard. "Don't let me throw up," I prayed silently, "please don't let me throw up."

Williams sighed. "You're sure? It couldn't have just been some old clothes or something?"

Parker shook his head. "It was a dead man," he insisted. "He was in the water, but I saw his face. It was, it was . . ."

For the first time, Parker faltered. He looked at me, and, despite all my efforts, I threw up my Twinkies, right there in the middle of the police station.

Williams pressed a buzzer under his desk, and a cop in the office behind a glass window opened a door and stuck his head out. "What's up?"

"Get a mop, Scruggs," Williams said. "Then send a car out to Fulton Farm Road. These boys claim there's a dead man in Indian Creek under the bridge."

While Scruggs cleaned up the mess I'd made, Williams took us into an office and got our names and addresses and ages. Then he asked us to tell him exactly where we'd camped and when we'd started walking up the creek and what we'd seen.

"Well, the first thing we saw was Mr. Evans," Parker said.

"Mr. Evans?" Williams paused, pencil poised.

"George Evans. He runs the Olde Mill Antique Shoppe on the corner of Windsor Road." Parker leaned toward the policeman as if he were trying to read what he was writing. "He was on the bridge, just standing there."

"Did he see you?"

"I don't know. We were pretty far away."

"How can you be sure it was him?"

Parker showed Williams his binoculars. "We were searching for a blue heron I've seen on that part of the creek," he said. "Then Otis started barking. I looked up, and I saw Evans on the bridge."

"Otis?"

"My dog." Parker nudged Otis with his foot and the dog thumped the floor with his tail.

Williams sighed. "Then what happened?"

"I pulled Otis back in the bushes with us and Mr. Evans got in his car and drove away. Then we walked on up the creek and Otis ran ahead. He started barking again, and when I caught up with him he had ahold of the dead man's shirt, kind of tugging at it. At first, I thought it was just rags, you know? But then I saw his face."

"And where were you all this time?" Williams looked at me a little reluctantly. He was probably afraid I'd throw up again.

"Armentrout was behind me," Parker answered. "By the time he caught up, I'd pulled Otis off the guy."

"But you did see the body," Williams said to me.

I nodded.

"And you agree it was a dead man."

I nodded again. "Yes, sir," I said.

The policeman tapped his pencil thoughtfully on his desk. "Had you ever seen the man before?"

I shook my head. "No, sir."

"He looked kind of familiar to me," Parker put in.

Before Williams could ask Parker anything else, the door buzzed and another policeman came in. "Can I speak to you in private, sir?" he asked.

Leaving Parker and me sitting by his desk, Sergeant Williams followed the other cop into another office. Through the glass window we watched them talking.

"I wish I could read lips," Parker whispered.

But since we couldn't, we just sat there and waited for Williams to come back. When he did, he wasn't smiling. He sat down and looked at us.

"Well, boys, it looks like you were right. There was a dead man in the creek, just where you said he'd be."

"Who was he?" Parker asked.

Williams shook his head. "No identification." He scratched his nose and gave Parker a speculative look. "Didn't you say he looked familiar to you?"

Parker nodded. "But I don't know why."

Williams stood up. "Well, if you think of anything, come see me." He shook Parker's hand, then mine. "Thanks for reporting the body. If you hadn't seen him, it might have been a while before anybody came across him, now that fishing season's over and deer season hasn't started."

"He was murdered, wasn't he?" Parker asked. "Shot between the eyes, right?"

"That's not for me to say." Williams gave Parker a small card with his name on it and told him again to try to remember where he'd seen the man.

"What about Mr. Evans?" Parker wanted to know. "Are you going to bring him in for questioning?"

Sergeant Williams pulled a pipe out of his desk drawer and busied himself lighting it. As he escorted us out of his office, he said, "Take my advice, Parker Pettengill, and let the police handle this."

·5·

FFICER SCRUGGS, the same policeman who'd cleaned up the mess I'd made, was waiting for us on the sidewalk outside the station. "Get in the car, boys," he said. "I'll take you home."

Parker, Otis, and I climbed in the backseat of the squad car. It took us a while to get Otis settled; riding in cars always excites him, and I could see Officer Scruggs frowning at us in the rearview mirror. I had a feeling he wasn't too happy about the way his Sunday was going.

"Aren't you going to turn on the siren or the lights?" Parker asked as Scruggs pulled away from the curb.

"This isn't an emergency, sonny." Scruggs didn't even glance at us. He just headed down Main Street toward Windsor Road, looking straight ahead.

"That guy was shot, wasn't he?" Parker leaned forward and gripped the back of Scruggs's seat. "I saw the bullet hole."

"I'm not at liberty to discuss the case with you." Scruggs turned the corner so fast Parker fell back against Otis who said "whuff" loudly enough to merit a look in the rearview mirror.

"Have you ever shot anybody?" Parker asked Scruggs.

The policeman didn't answer, but I could see he was getting mad. Maybe Parker noticed, too, because he pressed his face against the car window and stared at the houses on Windsor Road as if he'd never seen them before. I think he was hoping somebody would notice him in the police car but everybody must have been sleeping or something. The only person we passed was old Miss Perkins. She was walking her little dog Tootsie, and she didn't even look up when Otis banged his muzzle against the window and barked.

When Officer Scruggs pulled up in front of my house, Parker and Otis followed me out of the car. "What kind of gun is that?" Parker was staring at the pistol Scruggs wore. "How many bullets are in it?"

As usual, Scruggs said nothing. Maybe he was the silent type, like Clint Eastwood in those Dirty Harry movies. Or maybe he just didn't like Parker and me.

When Mom opened the door, she looked like she was going to faint right there in front of us. She must have thought we'd been arrested or something, but Officer Scruggs soon set her straight.

After he was sure Mom and Dad understood what

had happened, he led Parker and Otis back to his car. It was his duty to talk to Pam, I heard him tell Parker as he opened the rear door and Otis jumped happily inside.

Well, after they left, you can imagine the scene in my house. Mom was crying and hugging me, saying she'd never let me go camping in the woods again, and Dad was trying to blame the whole thing on Parker.

"I always knew that boy would get you into trouble," he kept saying. "He's never been anything but a bad influence on you." Then he was off, remembering every awful thing Parker and I had done since we first met in kindergarden.

"Oh, Donald," Mom finally said, just as Dad was remembering the time Parker dared me to jump off the high dive before I'd learned to swim.

"Matthew could have drowned," Dad said.

"Parker didn't know I couldn't swim," I said, "and, besides, the lifeguard was right there, wasn't he?"

Luckily for me Charity appeared at that moment and demanded to know what was going on. "Did I see a police car out front?" she asked. "Is Matthew going to jail?"

While Charity made a pest of herself trying to get some answers to her questions, Mom and Dad forgot me for a while and argued about my camping equipment and my bike instead. Mom was all for leaving them at Indian Creek forever.

"No one in this family is going anywhere near that place," she said. "Who knows where the murderer is. He could still be lurking about, just waiting to strike again."

But Dad wouldn't listen to her. He hopped in the station wagon and drove out there all by himself, gathered up everything, even Parker's stuff, and brought it back home.

By the time Dad returned, we had another visitor, a reporter from the *Woodcroft Sentinel*. Accompanied by Parker and Otis, Julius Fisk appeared at the door, laden with cameras, a tape recorder, and notebooks. He was trying to persuade Mom to let us go out to Indian Creek for some pictures.

"It's perfectly safe," he told Mom. "The police are all over the place, doing their scene-of-the-crime routine. I just want a few shots of the boys pointing at the creek. A little human interest, nothing more."

Although I wasn't at all excited about going to Indian Creek, Dad thought it was a good idea. "Matthew should see the police in action," he told Mom. "It will be reassuring for him to realize how quickly things return to normal."

So, thanks to Dad, I found myself sharing the backseat of Julius Fisk's small car with Otis while Parker rode up front, pointing things out to Fisk and filling him in on all the details of our morning.

"And then Armentrout threw up," Parker concluded. "You never saw such a mess."

As he described the scene, I scowled at the back of Parker's head and slumped a little lower in the seat. I just didn't see why he had to tell Fisk that. With my luck, the entire account would be in the paper for everyone to read and laugh at. Some friend, I thought.

We got to Indian Creek just as the rescue squad was carrying the dead man up the hill in one of those orange plastic body carriers you see sometimes on the evening news. As they slid the man into the ambulance, I wondered who he was and if anybody was worrying about him. It seemed so awful to end your life like that.

After Fisk had taken a few pictures of the rescue squad, he made Parker and me show him exactly where we found the body. The water was dark and still beneath a gloomy sky, and it scared me to go under the bridge again. Fisk kept firing questions at Parker and me. "How did the dead man look? Could you really see the bullet hole? Were you scared? Did you see anybody else? Did you notice anything suspicious? Do you plan to camp here again?" And on and on. His voice bounced off the bridge and echoed in my ears till I felt dizzy.

Although Parker was excited and eager to talk, he didn't say a word about Evans. Since I thought the creep's presence on the bridge was just a coincidence, I didn't mention him either. In fact, I kind of faded into the background and let Parker take over. He always was better at talking to people than I was.

By the time Julius Fisk drove us home it was almost five o'clock and I hadn't had anything to eat since the horrible Twinkies. I was tired and I was hungry, and all I wanted to do was have dinner and go to bed.

*

Later, Mom came in to say good night. "Is everything okay, Matt?" she asked. "That reporter didn't upset you, did he?"

I shook my head. "The whole thing was just kind of scary, that's all," I said. "A dead man, you know, really dead. Shot in the head. I never in my whole life expected to see anything like that."

Mom patted my hand. "Certainly not here in Woodcroft." She folded her arms across her chest and shivered a little.

I looked around my room. My model airplanes dangled from the ceiling, moving a bit in a draft from the window, and the glow from my fish tank illuminated a poster of Sylvester Stallone in his Rambo getup. Somewhere out there in the darkness beyond my windows was a murderer, and I wasn't going to feel safe again until he was in jail.

As Mom stood up, I grabbed her hand to stop her from leaving. "George Evans was on the bridge. Parker and I saw him just before we found the body."

"What could George have been doing there?" Mom sounded puzzled.

"Parker thinks he killed that man and threw him into the creek."

Mom stared at me. "For heaven's sake, Matthew,

that's the silliest thing I've ever heard. George is a very nice person."

I sat straight up, almost too shocked to speak. "You think Evans is *nice*?"

"Matthew, what's gotten into you? George has been very generous to this town. Why, he donated several hundred dollars to the high school band when he heard they needed new uniforms, and he also contributed a great deal to the fund drive for the new library. I can't believe Parker would say such a terrible thing."

"If Evans didn't have anything to do with the dead man, what was he doing on the bridge?"

"I'm sure there's an explanation, Matt," Mom said. "He could have been jogging or just walking, who knows? You and Parker were both there too—do you think anyone suspects you?" She laughed and gave me a little hug.

Then she drew back and thought a moment. "Isn't Pam dating George?"

"How did you know?"

"Woodcroft is a small town," Mom said. "It's common knowledge he's taking her out."

"Well, so what if he is? What's that got to do with anything?"

"You know how Parker feels about his mother." Mom patted my hand. "Don't you think he might be a little jealous?"

When I didn't answer, she added, "In other words, Parker could be trying to make George look bad, honey. Just bear that in mind, and don't let your imagination run away with you." She gave me a quick kiss. "Now you get some sleep," she said. "I'm sure you need it."

As Mom closed the door behind her, I slid down in bed and wondered about what she'd said. Was that the explanation? Parker was jealous of Evans?

But there was more to it, wasn't there? We'd seen Evans on the bridge—or had we? After all, the morning had been foggy. Maybe Parker had just thought it was Evans. True, the car had sounded like the MG, but it could have been some other car with a bad muffler.

While I tried hard to remember every detail of the man's appearance on the bridge, a branch scratched against my window, making a sound like a bony hand knocking on the glass. Once again, I saw the dead man's face under the water, his hair floating around his head like weeds. Pulling the covers up to my chin, I rolled over and shut my eyes. I wasn't going to think about Evans or the dead man or anything else. I was going to fall asleep and forget it all.

# ·6·

**L**ATER THAT NIGHT I woke up moaning from a nightmare. Parker and I were at the creek again, but this time the dead man got up from the water, all dripping and horrible, and started chasing us. It was one of those dreams where you try to scream but you can only go "Uh uh," and you try to run but you can only hobble.

Lying there with my heart thumping, I thought I heard somebody creeping up the stairs—the dead man maybe, or Evans—and I was too scared to move. I just watched the door and wished I'd locked it. Then a breeze billowed the curtains, and I thought Evans was trying to climb through my window. Telling myself to grow up, I squeezed my eyes shut, but the dead man kept flashing in front of me, staring at me with those awful eyes.

Turning over on my stomach I pressed my face into

my pillow. If only Parker and I had never gone camping at Indian Creek.

*

Monday morning, I picked up the *Woodcroft Sentinel* and almost lost my appetite for breakfast. The murder was on the front page, along with a picture of Parker pointing at the place where we'd found the dead man. I was standing beside him looking fat and sad, and Otis was in the background. Julius Fisk had garbled everything Parker and I told him, so we sounded kind of stupid in print. To make it even worse, he put in a detailed description of me throwing up in the police station, just as I had feared he would. As a result, Parker came out the hero, while I was the comic relief.

The only thing I learned from the article was that Parker was right. The man really had been shot in the head with a small caliber bullet. But nobody knew who he was or where he came from. The police suspected he had been killed somewhere else and dumped in Indian Creek. In fact, Sergeant Williams was quoted as saying it looked like a drug war execution.

"Drugs," Mom said. "Can you imagine? That's the kind of thing that happens in Washington or Baltimore, not in a nice little town like this."

I shoveled some cereal in my mouth and tried to choke it down. There were a lot of things Mom didn't know about Woodcroft, I thought. If I was the kind of kid who wanted drugs, I knew a dozen places to get them.

"What's the matter, Matthew?" Mom watched me shove my cereal aside, half eaten. "Don't you feel well?"

I tried to convince her I was too upset about the dead man to go to school, but I ended up slogging to Letitia B. Arbuckle Junior High through a cold drizzle. The wind was blowing a bunch of ragged clouds across the sky, and wads of leaves eddied around in the air and slapped down on the sidewalk, all wet and slimy.

It was the dreariest day of the year, and when I met Parker on the corner, he looked just as miserable as I felt. The rain had plastered his hair against his skull, and his eyes were shadowed. I had a feeling he hadn't slept any better than I had.

"Do you think everybody at school saw the paper?" I asked him.

Parker nodded. "We'll be famous," he said, but he didn't sound particularly excited.

"They'll all know I threw up. Why did you have to tell Fisk about it?"

"I didn't think he'd put it in the article," Parker said.

I sighed. Not too far ahead of us, I saw Jennifer Irwin and her friends, Linda Greene and Melissa Woltzman. Jamming my hands in my back pockets like Parker, I slowed down. If there was one person I hoped hadn't read the article it was Jennifer. I've been half in love with her since she kissed me in third grade; unfortunately, she's never done it again, but I keep hoping. Who wouldn't?

Parker didn't seem to notice how slowly I was walking. Head bent, he was thinking his own thoughts, so I was free to admire Jennifer's long blond braid swinging just below her waist and the way she tilted her head when she talked and the sound of her laugh floating back to me.

Much as I would have liked to catch up with Jennifer and see her smile, I let the distance between us grow. For one thing, I never had the nerve to say more than "hi" to her, and after I'd said that I'd have to walk on past her. Then, instead of me seeing her back, she'd see mine.

But even worse, if she'd read the paper, she'd probably have a million questions about the dead man, and it would be Parker she'd be talking to, not me. And worst of all, she might tease me about my performance in the police station. If Jennifer didn't, I knew Linda and Melissa would. Especially Linda—she's the kind of girl who just loves to make a fool out of you.

So I dawdled along until Parker finally noticed our snaillike pace. By then we were only a block away from school, and Jennifer, Melissa, and Linda were waiting on the corner ahead of us for two other girls in our class.

"We're going to be late, Armentrout," he said.

"What do you want? Detention with Miklowitz?"

Parker hurried ahead and caught up with the girls as they started to cross the street. Just as I thought, he was immediately surrounded and bombarded with questions about the dead man. Like a rock star being interviewed by his fans, Parker turned from one to the other, giving each of them a few details. Until Linda asked me about throwing up, nobody even looked at me. Then, of course, they all started laughing and making fun of me.

All except Jennifer. "If I saw a dead man I'd throw up too," she said. "Just like Matt."

After that, I didn't care what Linda said or did. Ignoring her, I pushed my way through the crowds in the hall, stuffed my jacket into my locker, and went to homeroom on my own little cloud.

All day I had to tell the story of the dead man over and over again. Even to my teachers. By the end of sixth period, I was sick of Indian Creek and eager to go home and forget about it.

When I met Parker in the hall, he said, "Let's get out of here." I could tell he was just as tired of being a celebrity as I was.

"Why don't we go to the quarry and work on our fort?" I suggested. The clouds had blown away, and the sun was shining again. Out in the woods, we'd be all alone. No questions to answer, no more teasing about throwing up, no more worries about the dead man.

\*

We went home long enough to pick up our bikes and Otis. Then we rode about two miles out of town to Bluestone Quarry. It was abandoned years ago, sometime before World War II, so it's way back in the woods and full of water now. There are "No Trespassing" signs posted along the road, but everybody swims in it anyway, even though it's real murky and cold as ice. Kids say it's bottomless. If you drown in it, they say, your body will never be found.

You can imagine what my parents would do if they knew Parker and I started building a fort there last summer. To hear them talk, you'd think a kid drowned in the quarry every day. Once in a while, maybe every ten years or so, somebody does drown, but Parker and I are very careful. And we always bring Otis with us for a little extra protection.

Actually the worst thing about the quarry isn't the water. Parker and I are pretty sure teenagers do drugs and stuff in the woods. Sometimes we find charred logs where they've had fires and beer cans and whiskey bottles lying around. The rocks are covered with the names of weird rock bands and drug sayings, sprayed on with black paint.

Once we saw a gray van parked way back in the woods. There were some motorcycles lying around and guys smoking joints, so Parker and I didn't work on our fort that day. We dragged Otis away before he started barking and went home.

Today, though, the woods were all ours, golden yellow and red, smelling like fall. A woodpecker was banging his brains out, hammering away at the trunk of a tree, the quarry water was blue and sparkling, and a cool breeze rustled through the leaves.

We worked on the fort for a while. The main part is sort of a dugout, with stone walls and a roof of boards we found at a construction site. Right now it's big enough for two people, if you don't stand up, and a dog. We're planning to enlarge it, but that afternoon Parker wanted to finish our defense system.

It was his idea to surround the fort with traps. Even though it was camouflaged with dead leaves and branches, he was worried the motorcycle guys would notice it and decide to use it themselves.

"We'll dig holes," he announced one day last summer. "And cover them with sticks and stuff. You know, like the pits they catch tigers in."

Actually I think he just wanted an excuse to dig. From the time he was little, Parker has been the kind of kid who mines his backyard with holes and tunnels. He loves the smell of dirt and roots and stones and can spend hours underground.

I prefer sunshine and fresh air myself, so my hole was only waist deep, but Parker's was already over his head and just wide enough for him and a shovel.

After an hour or so, I heard Parker yell something. Hoisting myself out of my hole, I walked over to his. There he was looking up at me. He must have dug down more than six feet, and he couldn't get out without my help.

As I pulled him up I started laughing.

"What's so funny?" Parker wanted to know.

"All you need is a honey jar on your head," I told him, "and you'd look like Pooh in the heffalump trap."

"Ha, ha," Parker said. I could tell he wanted me to take his work seriously. He was covered with mud and his jeans and shoes were soaked from the rainwater in the bottom of the hole.

Like a mining engineer, he studied his excavation. "Do you think it's deep enough?"

"Another week and you'll be shaking hands with the Chinese," I said.

"Be serious, will you?" Parker started gathering little sticks and laying them over the hole. "Come on, Armentrout," he muttered, "get some leaves and help me cover it up."

When Parker was finally satisfied, we sat down on a boulder near the fort. With the sun shining down through the thinning leaves, it was just like old times—until Parker suddenly turned to me and said he remembered where he'd seen the dead man.

# ·7·

"REMEMBER THAT DAY last summer when we were going to work on the fort but your mother made you go the dentist instead?" Parker asked.

I nodded. As soon as school let out in June, Mom was always dragging me off somewhere horrible. The dentist, the allergist, the math tutor. If it were up to her, my whole vacation would be spent in boring air-conditioned offices, little boxes where somebody is always poking needles in your arm or adjusting your braces or drilling you on fractions and percentages.

"Well, I rode my bike out here anyway," Parker said. "Just me and Otis. And I saw that gray van again. The guys on the motorcycles were sitting around like before, smoking dope and drinking beer."

He looked up from the stick he'd been whittling. As usual, his hair almost hid his eyes and he had to toss it back to see me. "The dead man was in the van. I saw his face when he left." Parker paused. "Of course, he wasn't dead then."

"No," I said, trying to sound sarcastic, but Parker didn't notice.

"I was hiding in the woods, right over there behind that tree." He pointed and Otis ran off, thinking Parker was throwing something for him to fetch. The poor dog sniffed around, even pawed at the dead leaves, and finally came back with a stick Parker must have thrown last week.

"He was real close, Armentrout, not more than a few yards away," Parker said.

I raised one eyebrow, a skill I've worked hard to develop. "Come on, Parker," I said. "You think the dead man is some guy you got a glimpse of way last summer?"

Parker frowned and threw the stick for Otis. "There was another man driving the van, older, kind of slick-looking."

He paused for a moment, his frown deepening. Suddenly he snapped his fingers and leaned toward me. "I've seen him too!" he said. "You know where? At the Olde Mill!"

"So?" I said. "Lots of people buy antiques there."

Parker tossed his hair back, too excited by his own thoughts to pay any attention to all the cold water I was throwing at him. "What if Evans is involved in some kind of drug thing?" he asked.

"You've been watching too much TV," I told him. Why couldn't he just forget about the dead man? It was a nice afternoon, and I wanted to enjoy the sun while it lasted. Before long it would be too cold to lounge around in the woods like this.

Parker straightened up and glared at me. "Just listen to me, Armentrout, will you? A few nights ago, I went over to the shop, looking for Pam. I was walking up to the back door when Evans came out with another man. They talked for a few seconds, the man put some boxes in the back of a snazzy-looking BMW, and then he left. I'm sure it was the same guy I saw driving the van."

"So what's that got to do with drugs?"

Parker sighed as if I were too stupid to talk to. "Don't you see? The guys in the van are dealers. We've seen them here in the woods selling stuff."

"But where does Evans fit in?" I was thinking about what Mom had said. Maybe Parker was so jealous of Evans that he was making up stuff about him, first thinking he was a murderer, now thinking he was a drug dealer.

"It's just a feeling I have," Parker said. "The boxes could've had something in them, I don't know." His voice trailed off, and he started picking at the frayed edge of a hole in his jeans.

For a while neither of us said anything. Otis gnawed his stick, growling softly, and the woodpecker continued to hammer away. The sun was sinking down behind the trees, and the air was cooling fast. To my embarrassment, my stomach rumbled loudly, reminding me it was time for dinner.

"So what are you going to do?" I asked Parker as we pedaled slowly home.

He chewed his lower lip thoughtfully. "Keep an eye on Evans, see what I can find out."

"You could tell Sergeant Williams," I said.

Parker shook his head. "We need more evidence, Armentrout." He sat back on his seat, hands in his pockets as we coasted down a hill. "We'll go over to the Olde Mill tonight, okay? I'll come by around nine and get you."

Before I could say yes or no, Parker turned the corner and sped away toward his house, hunching low over the handlebars like a racer.

*

True to his word, Parker showed up at quarter to nine. Luckily Mom was too busy helping Charity with her homework to notice me leaving the house. Dad didn't notice either; as usual, he was in his study doing something with his computer.

Before we'd gone two blocks, we heard the clink clink of dog tags behind us. It was Otis, of course.

Parker glared at him. "How did you get loose?"

Otis barked and wagged his tail, then ran on ahead, circling back every now and then to make sure we were still behind him.

"No matter where I go," Parker said, "he tracks me down. I just can't get away from that dog."

When we got to the Olde Mill, the shop was dark. In the moonlight, the chrysanthemums in the barrels flanking the front door were the color of blood, and the tiny panes of glass in the windows glinted dully. The old-fashioned sign, hand-painted by Pam, creaked as a little gust of wind sent a swirl of leaves dancing across the deserted parking lot. With its stone walls and green shutters, the shop looked like a fairy-tale cottage, not the sort of place anyone would expect to find drugs or murder.

"There's nobody here," I whispered to Parker.

"He lives in the back," Parker said. "Come on, we'll sneak around the corner and look in the workroom windows."

"Are you sure we shouldn't just go to the police?" I knew I was being a coward, but I couldn't help it.

"Are you kidding?" Parker stared at me. "Who'd believe us? You know what a model citizen Evans is, giving money to the high school and the library and all. Like I told you, we have to get some proof."

Then, warning Otis to be quiet, Parker led me around back. Squeezing between a bush and the wall, we edged up to a window and peeked in.

The first thing we saw was Pam. She was sitting at a worktable cleaning the face of an old doll. At first, I thought she was alone, but after a few minutes Evans came into the room. While Parker and I watched, he put his arm around her. Then he bent down and kissed her, a long kiss, the kind that makes you sick in movies when they show it up close and you can see teeth and lips and neck muscles and stuff.

Next to me, Parker cursed, the worst words I'd ever heard him say, but I didn't blame him. I felt like swearing myself.

Finally Evans straightened up. Hefting the doll, he tilted it back and forth, grinning. Pam looked up at him and said something. She was frowning, but Evans just shrugged, patted her head, and laid the doll down on the table. Then he started kissing her again.

Parker muttered a few more terrible curse words and backed away from the window. His face was pale and angry in the light streaming through the dirty glass.

At that moment, Otis scared up a cat from somewhere and started chasing it across the gravel parking lot, barking loudly. Immediately the back door opened and Evans was standing there, frowning at us.

"I came by to get my mother," Parker said, walking right up to him.

Evans didn't step aside. He stood where he was, blocking the doorway, and Pam joined him.

"Parker, what are you doing here?" she asked. In all honesty, she didn't look pleased to see us.

"I was just getting a little hungry," Parker said, "and I was wondering when we were having dinner, that's all."

Parker was trying hard to sound sarcastic, but I knew he was upset. And who could blame him? This late and no dinner? I'd eaten at six, a big helping of steak and potatoes, salad, and chocolate ice cream, and I was already starving again.

"I told you I had to work late, honey." Pam squeezed around Evans to see us better. "I left a frozen pot pie in the freezer. Didn't you see it?"

"I don't call that dinner," Parker said.

Evans reached into his pocket and hauled out a moneyclip stuffed full of bills. Selecting a twenty, he offered it to Parker. "Get yourself something at the Dairy Queen," he said. "Your Mom's helping me with an important shipment."

Parker ignored the money and Evans. "Come on, Pam," he said. "Let's go home."

"Honey, you heard what George said." Pam's voice had a pleading tone that reminded me of Charity trying to wheedle a favor out of Dad. "Take the money and treat yourself and Matthew to something nice. Banana Loveboats or triple scoop cones."

While Pam and Parker stared at each other, Otis ran back into the parking lot. At the sight of Evans he growled deep in his throat, and Parker grabbed his collar.

Evans frowned at the dog. "I forgot to congratulate you two on your appearance in the paper." He gave Parker and me a long, hard look.

Parker shrugged and busied himself petting Otis while Evans lit a cigarette. Exhaling a long, slow curl of smoke, he said, "It's getting so a man can't take an early morning ride without somebody reporting him to the police."

In the silence following this remark, I stole a quick look at Pam. She was leaning against the doorframe, and her hair was backlit so it glowed around her head like a halo. It was too dark to see the expression on her face, but I did notice her hand reach out and rest lightly on Evans's arm.

"Fortunately the police don't take kids very seriously," Evans added. "I guess you just got a little carried away playing detective, right?" He smiled now, one arm around Pam, the other hanging loose.

Pam shifted her position and the light over the door shone down on her face, bleaching it white, casting shadows over her eyes.

"Take the money, Parker," she said, "and get something to eat. I'll be home in an hour or so."

Without looking at either one of them or taking the money, Parker turned away. "Let's go Armentrout," he said.

Just once, when we were in the shadows on the sidewalk, I looked back. Evans had put the money into his pocket, and he and Pam were embracing again, their bodies black against the light behind them.

# ·8·

WALKING BACK TO my house, Parker and I didn't say much. Even Otis was kind of subdued. Instead of running in circles, sniffing everything, he just plodded along beside Parker, looking as glum as he did. Sometimes I think Otis picks up all of Parker's moods, reads his mind or something.

Finally I said, "Well, the van wasn't there."

"No." Parker kicked a stone and Otis chased it kind of halfheartedly. "Something's worrying Pam," he said. "Did you notice how tense she was?"

I nodded, remembering her face with the harsh light over the door shining down on it.

"Evans was pretty nervous, too," Parker added.

"At least the police took you seriously enough to talk to him," I said.

Parker glanced at me. "Just because we didn't see anything tonight doesn't mean Evans isn't involved," he said. "What about keeping the Olde Mill under surveillance?"

I started to make another joke about watching too many cop shows, but I stopped myself. Parker was looking at me like a little kid, anxious, worried, maybe even scared.

"For Pam's sake," he said before I had a chance to say anything.

"Pam?"

"If Evans murdered that guy, what about her? Either she knows something or she doesn't. Either way, she could be in danger."

We were standing still now, under a streetlight, staring at each other. All around us, the neat lawns of Woodcroft lay in shadow. Lamps and TVs glowed in windows, a car drove slowly past, its headlights sweeping bushes and trees, a few crickets chirped. Everything seemed so normal and safe and calm. Yet Parker and I were talking about murder and drugs and stuff. It seemed so unreal I wanted to laugh.

"Every day after school, we'll hide in the woods behind the shop and watch," Parker said. He wasn't joking. He meant it. "I don't want anything to happen to my mother."

*

So, for a week, Parker, Otis, and I spent our afternoons in the woods behind the Olde Mill. Both Otis and I would have preferred going to the quarry. Even digging heffalump traps was more fun than watching little old ladies coming and going with antiques. But we couldn't drag Parker away from the shop.

One afternoon, a woman got out of a Mercedes with Pennsylvania tags and went inside the shop. We heard the little bell over the door tinkle, and I imagined Evans stepping out of the back room, grinning his big grin, welcoming another blue-haired lady.

While I was dozing off waiting for her to come out, Otis growled, and Parker grabbed his collar. Our enemy had just stepped outside. We watched him carry an oak washstand to the Mercedes and lash it securely on the roof. When he was finished, the woman thanked him and drove away. Evans waved and went back inside.

"That furniture," Parker mused. "It could be packed with drugs. You know that?"

"No way," I said. "That lady is probably somebody's dear old granny."

Parker sighed and leaned back against a tree as if he were planning to fall asleep like Rip Van Winkle and wake up a hundred years from now. My stomach growled so loudly Otis cocked his ears and peered around, thinking, I guess, that some varmint was creeping up on him.

"It's almost five," I told Parker. "Do you want to have dinner at my house?"

"I'm always eating at your place," he said. "Are you sure your folks don't mind?"

I stood up and brushed leaves and dirt off my jeans.

Actually my father had complained when I first started bringing Parker home at dinnertime, but he was used to it now. And Mom usually went ahead and set an extra place without my even asking her to.

"They enjoy your company," I told him. "Otis, too."

We walked slowly through the woods, taking the shortcut behind the houses on Blake Street. Lights were on in the windows, and we could see families getting ready for dinner. In one brightly lit kitchen, I saw Jennifer Irwin helping her mother with something on the stove.

Parker saw her too, and he watched her till she moved out of sight. "Jennifer's the prettiest girl in school," he said.

"Do you like her?" I asked as we started walking again, scuffing the leaves up in yellow clouds.

Parker shrugged. "If I ever have a girlfriend, it'll be Jennifer."

Then he started running through the woods, yelling like an Indian, and I chased after him. Behind us, we could hear Jennifer's dog barking, but I wouldn't have cared if he'd bitten me in half. I'd never have a chance with Jennifer if Parker liked her, that was for sure.

"Not you again," Charity said when Parker sat down next to her. "Don't you ever eat dinner at your own house?"

Mom frowned at Charity. "We don't speak like that to guests," she said sternly.

Charity turned her attention to the meatloaf on her plate. "Not *this* again," she said loudly and glanced at Parker out of the corner of her eye to see if he was impressed. "I *hate* meat loaf."

I nudged her side. "Quit showing off," I said.

"Don't shove me." Charity pointed her knife at me like a sword. "Or I'll slice you up in pieces."

"Stop right there," Dad said. "Either eat your dinner or go to your room."

He made this threat every night, but it always solved the problem, at least temporarily. Charity bent her head over her plate and poked at her food, complaining loudly about everything from the onion in the meat loaf to the presence of peas on her plate.

"You know I hate peas and onions," she whined to Mom, but everyone ignored her. Her complaints were as much a part of meals at our house as the meat-and-potato diet Dad demanded. Charity sulked for a while, but she ended up eating everything except the bits of onion she dug out of the meat loaf. These she lined up neatly around the rim of her plate, positioning each one with the tines of her fork.

After two helpings of pumpkin pie and real whipped cream, Parker and I headed for my room to escape the nightly argument about cleaning up. As we climbed the steps, I could hear Charity complaining that I never did anything.

"It's your turn to wash the dishes," Mom said. "Matt washed them last night. It's right here on the kitchen calendar."

To drown out Charity's screeching countercharge, I slammed my bedroom door and turned on the stereo.

Parker flopped down on the bottom part of my bunk bed and started leafing through a *Mad* magazine. Thinking he must be sick to death of the constant bedlam at my house, I fiddled with the controls on the stereo, trying to increase the volume enough to drown out the noise in the kitchen but not enough to bring Dad to the door, yelling at me to turn it down.

After a while, Parker tossed *Mad* across the room and sighed.

"Coming over here must be a real drag," I said. "The way everybody shouts and carries on is enough to drive you nuts."

Parker glanced at me. "Actually, I was just thinking it's like being in one of those family shows on TV."

I stared at him. "Are you crazy? Those shows are funny, and the parents always know the right way to handle everything. Here it's just a mess of confusion."

Parker shrugged. "At least you have a family," he muttered. "Your mother cares enough about you to fix dinner for you every night."

There was a little silence then as the tape ended and began reversing itself. I didn't know what to say, so I was glad when the next song began and I could play with the tone and volume again.

Suddenly Parker jumped up so fast he bumped his head on the top bunk. "I better get going," he said.

I followed him downstairs. Charity was arguing with Mom about a new subject. "I don't want to study my spelling words," she was wailing. "I want to watch television."

If Mom hadn't been locked in a power struggle with a six-year-old, she might have stopped me with questions about homework, especially my book report.

But she didn't hear or see a thing, and Parker and I slipped out the back door like prisoners escaping from jail. Otis jumped up from the porch and ran ahead of us, his tail waving, and I had to hurry to keep up with Parker.

The air was thick with bonfire smoke, and a big orange harvest moon stared down at us from just above the treetops. Little gangs of leaves scurried this way and that, ankle deep on sidewalks that hadn't been raked.

"Are you going back to the Olde Mill?" I asked Parker as he turned down Blake Street.

"We've watched the shop every afternoon," he said, "and all we've seen are old ladies buying antiques. Maybe the real action is at night."

Holding on to Otis's collar, I followed Parker into the woods behind Jennifer's house. This time I didn't see her anywhere, and I wondered which one of the lighted windows was her bedroom. I imagined her sitting at a little desk with her homework spread out in front of her. Maybe she was working on her book report for Mr. Simpson, and I wished I were at home doing that instead of following Parker through the woods.

When we got to our hiding place, we peered out through the bushes at the Olde Mill. The back room was still lit, and very faintly I could hear a sad song about an unfaithful wife, the kind they always play on country music stations. Other than that, there was no sign of any action.

"How long are you planning to stay here?" I asked Parker after a while. My feet were cold and my legs were stiff from squatting. Pretty soon my parents were bound to notice my absence, and I'd get in trouble for going out on a school night without permission.

"At least till midnight." Parker looked at his watch's luminous face. "It's a few minutes past nine now. If you want to leave, go ahead. I'll be okay by myself."

I shivered as a gust of wind sent a shower of leaves down on our heads. In the woods all around us, branches swayed and creaked and things you couldn't see rustled and snapped in the dark. Clouds swirled past the moon, and I told myself I'd stay till ten, no later.

As I was checking my watch for the hundredth time, I heard a car coming down Windsor Road. It was Evans. Before he got out of the MG, the door of the shop opened, and Pam ran outside to meet him. They embraced, then turned and went inside. In a couple of minutes, the lights went out and everything was still.

"Let's go," Parker said. "We've seen enough."

Grabbing Otis, he told him roughly to be quiet. Then, without even bothering to say good-bye, Parker ran off toward his house, leaving me to stumble back home alone through the dark, cold woods.

## ·9·

AS A RESULT of my so-called sneaking out on a school night, I was grounded for the rest of the week. I wasn't even allowed to go to the library to pick out a book for my English assignment, so I had to read the only novel in our house, an old paperback of Mom's called *Flames of Desire*. Can you imagine being a seventh-grade boy and doing a book report like that?

If I hadn't been such a chicken, I would've followed Parker's example and not handed one in, but my parents stood over me and made sure I read every word of that stupid book. Mom said it would teach me a valuable lesson. When I asked her what it was, though, she just pursed up her mouth and gave me one of her looks.

Anyway, I had to stand up in front of the whole class, and tell about this beautiful lady who was kidnapped by pirates and fell in love with their captain even though he used her against her will. In a futile effort to make everybody laugh, I was hamming it up, but when I glanced at Jennifer, I noticed she was staring at Parker. He was gazing out the window like he was miles away from the rest of us.

The expression on Jennifer's face distracted me from my summary, and I stumbled over the word historical and said "hysterical" fiction instead. Even Mr. Simpson laughed then, which just goes to show you're funniest when you aren't trying to be.

I sat down and Melissa started droning on and on about her book, the story of a girl who loses weight to become a cheerleader. She must not have left out a single boring detail. Instead of listening to her, I watched Jennifer and Parker. Although he never noticed, she stared at him till it was her turn to give her book report. Even then, she kept stealing looks at him, but he was still gazing out the window.

*

Finally, Saturday came, Halloween at last, and all I had to do to earn my freedom was rake the leaves. Since Charity and Jennifer's little sister Tiffany kept jumping in the pile yelling, "I'm the Queen of the Universe," and scattering leaves all over the yard, it took me a long time. The minute I was through, I hopped on my bike and rode over to Parker's.

I was thinking he might want to go trick or treating after dark. I was pretty sure he hadn't gotten his Frankenstein costume together, but I'd left my Dracula outfit laid out on my bed. Surely Parker could fix himself up like a tramp or something.

As soon as I saw Parker, though, my dreams of candy bars and popcorn balls vanished. He was sitting on his front steps, one arm around Otis, looking totally miserable.

Skidding to a stop, I got off my bike and let it crash to the ground behind me. "What's wrong, Parker?"

"Nothing." Parker hugged Otis so tightly the dog made a little squeaking sound, but, loyal canine that he was, he thumped his tail and didn't try to pull away.

I plopped down beside Parker, and, for a few seconds, neither of us said a word. The only noise came from the leaves skittering across the porch behind me. I couldn't help noticing that nobody made Parker Pettengill do any raking.

Picking up a stone, Parker hurled it into a group of dented trashcans huddled together on the curb. Otis launched himself off the porch and ran after it. He snuffled around, found the stone, and brought it back to Parker. Dropping it, he cocked his head to one side and wagged his tail. His mouth was open, his tongue hung out, and he looked like a happy idiot, grinning at tragedies he didn't understand.

Parker threw the stone again, farther this time, and Otis charged off into the woods across the street, determined to make Parker happy.

"Pam didn't come home last night," Parker said at last.

Shoving my hands into the pockets of my denim

jacket, I didn't look at Parker, and I didn't say anything either. The truth was, I didn't want to hear about this kind of stuff.

But Parker kept talking. "When I asked her what was going on, she blew up," he said. "She started yelling at me about the shop and all the work she had to do and my attitude. She never acted like this till she got involved with Evans."

As Parker stared dejectedly into space, I wished I knew how to cheer him up. But what could I say? Pam had changed. Just last summer, she and Parker and I played ball in the backyard, chasing each other around and laughing, or she drove us to Greenbriar State Park to swim in the lake. Oh, she'd had a few boyfriends, but Parker had always come first, anybody could see that.

Then Evans bought the Olde Mill, hired Pam, and now she was hardly ever home, and when she was she never laughed or kidded around like before.

Otis whimpered and nudged his stone against Parker's foot. This time I threw it, narrowly missing Pam's old Volkswagen.

"I'll tell you something," Parker said. "I'm going to find out what's going on."

I looked at him, but he was staring straight ahead. At the sound of a car coming down the street, we both looked up and watched it stop in front of the house. Pam got out and turned to say something to Evans. Otis growled and strained against his collar, wanting to chase the MG, but Evans didn't look at the dog or Parker and me. He just sped off, his nose in the air, a pipe jutting up out of his mouth.

Before Pam was halfway to the house, Parker sprang to his feet and went inside, leaving me sitting there all by myself, too surprised to follow him.

"Hi, Matthew." Pam smiled at me, and, even though I tried to harden my heart against her, it went flip-flop anyway.

"Where did Parker rush off to?" She stopped at the bottom of the steps, and her blue eyes, so much like Parker's, were level with mine.

She was wearing faded jeans and a baggy rag wool sweater, so big on her I thought it must belong to Evans. A pair of antique earrings dangled halfway to her shoulders, and her hair was a tangled lion's mane from riding in the MG with the top down.

"Parker's in the house," I said finally, but my voice cracked so the first words came out low and the others high. There was something about Pam that ruined all my efforts to sound like a man instead of a kid. She unnerved me almost as much as Jennifer did.

"I know that, Matt," Pam said, "but why did he disappear the minute he saw me?"

"I think he had to go to the bathroom," I said, and then my face got so red I jumped up and went inside to look for Parker before she asked me any more questions. Two dumb answers were enough for one day.

I found Parker in the kitchen trying to make grilled cheese sandwiches in a frying pan.

"You've got the heat too high," I said, eyeing the charred bread.

"I like them this way." Parker started scraping off the burned parts. "Want one?"

"No, thanks."

While Parker ate, I looked around the kitchen. With Pam away so much, the house was dirtier and dingier every time I came over. The sink was always full of dishes, and empty pizza boxes sat around for days with flies crawling on them. Even the plants on the kitchen windowsill were turning brown and losing their leaves.

For something to do, I picked up one of the dolls lying on the table and tilted her back and forth, watching her eyes open and shut. Without a wig, she had a big hole in the top of her head and you could look inside and see the mechanism that worked her eyes.

"Put that down, Matthew!" To my surprise, Pam entered the room and snatched the doll out of my hands. "These are very fragile," she added as she gathered up the dolls and laid them carefully in a large cardboard box.

"Armentrout was just looking at it," Parker said. "He wasn't going to hurt it."

Pam glanced at me as she pressed down the lid of the box. "I'm sorry, Matt," she said, "but your hands aren't very clean. Collectors pay a lot for a doll in good condition."

Parker frowned, but I was ready to crawl under the back porch like Otis does when he's in trouble. Then Pam patted my shoulder. "Don't mind me," she said, trying to smile. "I'm just a little edgy today."

Parker shoved his chair back and dumped the black remains of his sandwich in the garbage can.

"Are you going to be here for dinner?" he asked Pam. He wasn't looking at Pam or me. In fact, he had his head in the refrigerator, searching for something. His voice was muffled, but his back had a rigid set to it as if he were tensed for bad news.

"George and I are going into Baltimore tonight. He's meeting an old friend, and we won't be back till late. I'll leave you enough money to send out for pizza." Pam didn't raise her eyes from the fingernail she was fixing with one of those little sticks women use for stuff like that, but her voice had a nervous edge. She looked tense too, as if she might jump up and run any minute.

There was a long silence. The refrigerator shuddered and started humming, and a gust of wind rattled the back door. Out in the yard, I could see Otis checking the bushes for rabbits or stones, I don't know which.

"You just got home." Parker shook the can of root beer he'd found. Then he popped the top and watched the root beer geyser up. When it hit the ceiling, he smiled to himself, but he didn't share the joke with anybody.

"Don't do that," Pam said sharply. "You're making a mess."

"Who'd notice?" Parker asked. "The way this place looks."

"I know you're mad," Pam said, "because I'm going out again, but tonight is important, and I have to be there. Can't you understand?" Her voice rose a little and her face flushed. "Believe me, I'd much rather stay right here!"

"Then why don't you?"

"It's my business, not yours."

"What are you and Evans up to anyway?" I could see a vein in Parker's neck sticking out like a knotted cord, and he was gripping the soda can so tightly the sides were bending in.

"That's enough, Parker!" Pam threw the little stick down and it bounced off the table onto the floor. She was so angry she scared me. With her hair in her face and her long nails curved like talons, she reminded me of one of those Furies in Greek myths.

But she didn't scare Parker. Like her, he was on his feet leaning toward her, and for the first time I realized he was as tall as she was. They could almost have been twins facing each other across the kitchen table.

Parker slammed the soda can down. "I wish we'd found Evans's body in Indian Creek!" he yelled.

Tears sprang to Pam's eyes. "You just don't understand anything, do you?" Snatching up the box of dolls, she ran from the room.

"Lord, Parker," I said as Pam's bedroom door slammed shut, "what made you go and say a thing like that?"

Parker didn't answer. He flopped down in a chair and put his head on his folded arms. From where I was standing, I could see the white nape of his neck and the frayed label inside the collar of his old plaid shirt.

Then his shoulders started shaking with sobs, and I didn't know if I should leave or stay. What did he want me to do? I couldn't ask him, and I couldn't think of anything to say. I wished I could make all the stuff he and Pam had said go away, like a teacher erasing words from a blackboard.

Suddenly Parker jumped up and went to the kitchen window. With his back to me, he said, "Would your mother let you spend the night over here?"

"I guess so."

Wheeling around, Parker stared at me. His face was flushed, but he'd gotten himself under control. Lowering his voice even though Pam was in the shower, he said, "We'll go to the Olde Mill and find out what's going on. Okay?"

# ·10·

B Y THE TIME I got home, Mom was in the middle of packaging her ornaments for the Fall Festival. When I asked her if I could spend the night at Parker's, all she said was to be home before noon on Sunday. "I'm counting on you to help at the booth tomorrow."

Then, just as I was getting ready to leave, she added, "Don't stay out too late trick and treating, Matt. Whoever murdered that man is still loose."

With those cheerful words ringing in my ears, I rode my bike back to Parker's house. As I skidded to a stop in the driveway, I saw Pam and Evans coming out the front door.

"Make sure Parker behaves himself." Pam smiled at me as if the scene in the kitchen had never taken place. "I know I can trust you to be sensible, Matt. No tricks, just treats. And don't eat too much candy."

I stood on the steps and watched her for a moment. She was wearing a long-sleeved blouse with a low, lacy neckline, and her dark flowered skirt swirled when she moved. As she turned to wave good-bye to Parker, her hair shone in the late afternoon sunlight. Then, her bracelets jingling, she took Evans's arm and walked down the sidewalk toward the MG.

Although Pam didn't seem to notice or even to care, Parker hadn't come to the doorway to wave to her, and Evans didn't say one word to me. His face expressionless, the man ignored both me and Otis who was barking furiously at him from the living room window.

The MG's engine kicked noisily into life and the two of them drove away, leaving the street duller and quieter as they vanished down a tunnel of yellow leaves.

Parker came up behind me so silently he startled me. "She won't be back until late tomorrow, I bet," he said. "Maybe not till Monday."

"She's so beautiful," I said more to myself than him.

"That was one of her new outfits," Parker said as I followed him into the house. "Where's the money coming from for clothes like that? Or for all this other stuff?" His gesture took in the TV and the VCR as well as a leather reclining chair I hadn't noticed before. "She's in trouble, Armentrout, I know she is."

Glumly, I slumped on the old sofa and watched Parker turn on the VCR. In honor of Halloween, Pam had brought home three videos to keep us entertained, and Parker had one of them, *The Night of the*

*Living Dead,* ready to play. When I realized what it was, I groaned.

"We've seen this at least half a dozen times," I said.

"And it still scares you, right?"

"No," I lied, "it bores me to death. What else do you have?"

"*Friday the Thirteenth* and *Nightmare on Elm Street.*" Parker grinned. "What were you hoping for, *Bambi*?"

After the living dead had killed off just about everybody, Parker called the pizza place and ordered a large tomato and cheese with mushrooms, green peppers, meatballs, onions, and anchovies on top. Since the delivery man came to Parker's house pretty regularly, he got it to us in less than fifteen minutes.

"Those dead guys in the movie," Parker said after we'd devoured most of the pizza. "Didn't they remind you of the man we found in the creek?"

The man's face flashed before me, and I had to force myself to swallow my pizza. "Hey, Parker," I said, "not while we're eating."

He shoved the *Sentinel* at me. "Did you see this?" He pointed at an article about the murder. "They identified him. His name's Albert Dawson, and he's got a record as long as your arm. See? Drugs, assault, armed robbery, all kinds of parole violations."

I scanned the article, written, of course, by our old friend Julius Fisk. "The cops are still saying it's drug related and it doesn't have anything to do with Woodcroft. They think he just ended up here," I said.

Parker shook his head. "Well, we're going to prove the cops are wrong." Tossing his empty soda can into the trash, Parker grabbed his denim jacket. "It's time to go," he said.

Opening the kitchen door, he stood there a minute, staring at the trees behind his house. The sky was a pure deep black, and the stars shone so brightly and in such numbers, you would have thought you were in a planetarium.

"Couldn't we just go trick or treating instead?" I asked.

But Parker was already halfway down his back steps, whistling for Otis. The way that dog acted, he must've known Parker wanted to lock him in the house. Instead of coming, he plunged off into the shadows, barking like a lunatic. Even when Parker banged his food dish up and down on the porch railing, Otis wouldn't come.

"Darn that dog," Parker said and threw Otis's dish into the backyard.

Then the two of us ran off in the opposite direction from Otis, hoping to lose him. The last thing we wanted was to have him follow us out to the Olde Mill and start barking like last time.

Even though it was still early, most of the trick or treaters had come and gone, and the streets had an empty, late-night feeling. A breeze rattled the limbs of the trees and sent the last of the leaves scurrying down the sidewalk behind us. The sound they made had a spooky edge to it, and I found myself looking over my shoulder from time to time, just to make sure it was only leaves following us.

When somebody shouted Parker's name, I jumped like a startled rabbit before I realized it was Jennifer. With Melissa and Linda flanking her like halfbacks, she ran down Blake Street toward us. The three of them were dressed as hoboes, and their bags bulging with Halloween goodies flapped against their legs. Tiffany and Charity were scurrying along behind them, almost tripping over their long skirts and big bags.

"How much candy did you get?" Melissa asked breathlessly.

"They don't have any," Linda said. Her sharp little eyes never missed a thing. "They've probably been soaping car windows."

Ignoring her friends, Jennifer smiled at Parker and offered him her bag. "Want some?"

Parker stuck in his hand and pulled out a Hershey bar. "Thanks," he said.

"Don't give Matthew any," Melissa said. "He might throw up."

I glared at her, but, before I could think of anything to say, Jennifer thrust her bag at me.

"Have some, Matt," she said.

As I searched with my fingers for something as good as Parker's Hershey bar, Jennifer invited us to go trick or treating with her and the others. Obviously displeased, Melissa and Linda started whispering to each other, while Charity and Tiffany urged Jennifer to take them to Appleton Street immediately.

"Miss Goldberg always has good stuff," Tiffany shrilled.

"And Mrs. O'Malley gives bubble gum," Charity yelled before turning to me. "But not to boys," she said. "Just to pretty little girls like me and Tiffany."

I busied myself unwrapping a Baby Ruth bar and tried to ignore Charity. Maybe if we hung around long enough, Jennifer would offer us some more candy or Parker would agree to go trick or treating with her.

"Thanks for the invitation," I heard Parker tell Jennifer, "but we've got something else to do."

I opened my mouth to protest, but Parker was already walking toward Windsor Road, so I smiled at Jennifer and shrugged, hoping she'd realize it wasn't my idea to go running off. As I hurried after Parker, I heard Charity yell, "If you soap any cars, I'm telling Daddy!"

# ·11·

WHEN WE GOT THERE, the Olde Mill was dark, and the parking lot was empty. Behind it, the woods were an inky mass of shadows beneath the starry sky. The last crickets of the year were chirping softly, and from somewhere far away I heard a dog bark. Otherwise it was very quiet.

Parker ran noiselessly across the gravel and disappeared around the corner of the shop. Reluctantly I followed him about as silently as an elephant on the rampage. Parker would have made a good Indian, I thought. But not me. I was the kind who would have been left at camp to guard the women.

We tried the doors first, but they were locked, of course. Then Parker found a small window.

"Boost me up," he said.

"What if somebody comes along?" I glanced behind me at the empty parking lot. On the street, a car cruised past, but its headlights didn't reach us.

Parker grabbed the windowsill and tried unsuccessfully to pull himself up without my help. "Come on, Armentrout," he said. "Don't chicken out now."

"There might be a burglar alarm." I tried to see if there was any tape on the window or one of those little sensors.

"In a town like Woodcroft?" Parker asked. "Most people don't even lock their back doors."

Out of arguments but still scared, I gave him a boost, and he managed to shove the window open and then wiggle inside.

"Go to the back door," he told me. "I'll let you in."

While I waited for him to open the door, I heard another car coming. I crouched down, my heart thumping, but the car went on past.

"What are you doing?" Parker stood in the doorway looking down at me.

"Nothing," I muttered and edged around him into the silent shop.

It was really dark inside. Evans had the place jammed with big bureaus and trunks, china closets, huge wardrobes, umbrella stands with grotesque faces carved on them, tables, and glass-fronted cabinets full of dolls and toys.

In the narrow beam from Parker's pocket flashlight, all these things crowded around us, casting weird shadows. Our reflections jumped out at us from tilted mirrors, scaring me more than once, and the sagging floor creaked under our feet. It was like being in a fun house; you never knew what you'd see next—a lion from a carousel, a cigar-store Indian, or a life-size cut-out of Elvis.

"What are we looking for?" I whispered.

Parker didn't answer. He was trying to open the door to the back room where Evans and Pam repaired things.

"Damn," he muttered, jiggling the knob, "it's locked."

Putting my shoulder against the door like they do in movies, I shoved hard, but nothing happened except I got a pain in my arm.

Parker pushed me aside. "I can get it with my library card," he said.

I watched him stick the plastic card in the crack between the door and the frame and jiggle it around. In a couple of seconds, he had the door open.

"Where did you learn to do that?" I asked him.

"I'm always losing my house key and locking myself out," Parker said. "This gets me in every time."

He shone his light around the room and zeroed in on Pam's worktable. The box of dolls she'd taken out of the kitchen was lying there, and he opened it. Carefully he lifted out a doll and examined her. In his flashlight's beam, the doll stared at him, her eyes wide open. Although Pam had carefully repainted her face and repaired her clothing, she hadn't given her a new wig. In fact, all the dolls in the box were still bald.

"Quit breathing on me, Armentrout," Parker said

as he put the doll back into the box. "You smell like anchovies."

I stepped back, embarrassed. "No worse than you do," I muttered, but Parker was too busy opening another box of dolls to pay any attention to me.

These dolls were finished. Wearing wigs, clothes, and shoes, they lay as still as sleeping children. When Parker picked one up, her eyes didn't open.

"That's weird," he said, tilting the doll back and forth. "She's all fixed, except her eyes."

Putting her down, he tried another doll, but her eyes wouldn't open either. In fact, not one of the six dolls would wake up no matter how hard we rocked them back and forth.

Parker looked at me. "This is really strange." He grabbed one of the bald dolls and looked into the hole on top of her head. Then he tilted her back and forth. "Her eyes work," he said. "Why would the others be all packed up, ready to go, if they're broken?"

I shook my head. "We better get out of here, Parker," I said. The darkness was getting to me, and the shop made lots of funny sounds, creakings and squeakings like mice or maybe rats burrowing through all the old junk.

"I'm going to take one with me." Parker lifted a doll out of the box and stared at its sleeping face. It seemed to be dreaming something unpleasant, and I would have preferred to leave it where it was.

"They'll notice it's gone, Parker," I whispered. The flashlight was making strange shadows on the wall and ceiling. If we'd been characters in a movie, spooky music would be playing, and everybody in the audience would say, "Get out of there, boys, before it's too late."

"Anyway," I added, trying hard to make a joke, "aren't you kind of old to play with dolls?" Unfortunately, my voice refused to cooperate and every word cracked as it left my mouth.

Parker frowned at me. "You're scared, aren't you?"

I shook my head. "I just think we ought to leave everything the way we found it."

Parker put the lid on the box and started for the door, still carrying the doll. But before he reached it, we heard a car enter the parking lot.

"What do we do now?" I stared at Parker, too scared to move or even think.

Parker looked around the workroom. "Shut the door and make sure it's locked," he whispered. "Then hide. And for God's sake, be quiet."

As I closed the door, I heard another car pull into the parking lot, and then low voices approaching the shop—Pam, Evans, and somebody else.

Trying not to bump into anything in the dark, I wedged myself behind a large wardrobe standing catercornered in the darkest part of the room. I didn't know where Parker was, but, as I heard a key turn in the door, I hoped he was well hidden.

When the light went on, I shut my eyes; like an ostrich, I was trying to believe that if I couldn't see them, they couldn't see me.

"Where are the dolls?" the stranger asked.

Opening my eyes slowly, I peeked around the edge of the wardrobe, grateful for the shadows all around me. A couple of feet away, I saw Pam and Evans. Another man stood even closer, but his back was turned toward me. He was short and stocky, but he looked strong and his sports jacket was tight across the shoulders.

"One box is finished." Evans shoved the dolls toward him. "And the other is almost done."

"How long before it's ready?" the stranger asked.

"In just a few minutes." Pam sounded so nervous I wondered if she were scared of him. "All I have to do is fill the dolls' heads and glue their wigs on."

The floor creaked as she walked toward the wardrobe and unlocked it. On the other side of the thin board separating us, I heard her rummage around. Then she shut the doors again, locked them, and walked back to the table. While I watched, too scared to breathe, she began packing a doll's head with little bags of white powder.

All of a sudden the stranger looked up from the box he'd been examining. "There's only five dolls in here," he said.

"What are you talking about?" Pam asked. "I put six in before we left for dinner." Her voice shook a little, and she clutched the doll she was working on against her chest. Never had I seen a person look so frightened.

"Do you want to count them yourself?" The stranger leaned toward her and shoved the box across the table.

"There *are* only five." I could hear shock in Pam's voice as she turned to Evans.

"You wouldn't cheat me, would you, George?" The stranger asked. "We've been friends for a long time," he went on, "but I can't afford another partner like Dawson." The sound of his voice made me wish I could shrivel up into a little dustball and roll off into a corner.

"Are you kidding, Flynn?" Evans choked out a laugh. "I'd never try anything like that. Didn't I dump Dawson for you?"

"You made a great job of it too," the man named Flynn said sarcastically. "Almost getting caught by two kids."

There was a brief silence. Suddenly Evans snapped his fingers. "Parker!" He spoke so loudly I thought he'd found his hiding place, but then he went on, "I bet Parker's got the doll. He's been snooping around here all week."

I could practically feel his eyes X-raying through the furniture, searching for Parker and me.

"You don't expect me to believe that." Flynn leaned back against the wardrobe and it tilted, almost squashing me.

While he spoke, I heard Evans moving around the room, hunting for us. Why hadn't Parker listened when I told him not to take the doll?

"Don't blame this on my son," Pam said. "Leave

him out of it, George! He's got nothing to do with it!"

I held my breath as Evans checked a pile of crates near me. If Flynn hadn't been leaning on the wardrobe, squashing me against the wall, Evans would probably have seen me. As it was, he was so close I could have touched him.

Then, just when I thought my ribs would crack, Flynn stepped away, and the wardrobe swayed forward, freeing me to breathe again.

"You're saying Pam's son broke in here and took one of the dolls?" Flynn's voice was full of scorn as Evans returned to the worktable without seeing me. "Don't kid me. You just wanted a little more than your share. A new house, a new car, a fancy cruise, something you couldn't quite afford."

"I'll get the doll," Evans said. "Just give me some time."

"You better," Flynn said. "You know as well as I do what it's worth. I can't afford to lose five thousand because I trusted a greedy fool."

"Come on, Pam," Evans said. "Let's get Parker."

"Pam stays here with me," Flynn said. "You go find the kid by yourself."

"Parker doesn't know anything about the cocaine," Pam said to Flynn as the door slammed behind Evans. "He's only twelve years old. He couldn't possibly be any danger to you."

Except for the sound of Pam crying, the shop was silent for a long time. Then I heard the MG, and in a few seconds, Evans was back.

"Nobody was home except that damn dog," he said. "He almost tore my leg off."

"Do you have any idea where the boy might be?" Flynn asked.

"He's got a fort out near Bluestone Quarry," Evans said. "He could be there, or he could be at his friend Matthew's house."

"I'll drive," Flynn said to Evans. "You make sure Pam behaves herself."

Gripping Pam's arm, Evans followed Flynn. The last thing I heard her say was, "Promise you won't hurt Parker." Then the shop door slammed shut, and we were alone in the darkness.

# ·12·

As soon as I thought it was safe, I stumbled out from behind the wardrobe. My legs were so stiff and cramped I could hardly walk, and the room was pitch black. I bumped right into Parker before I realized who it was.

"Where were you?" I whispered. "I was sure they'd find us."

"I was lying down behind that pile of boxes." Parker pointed to a dark corner. "Evans was about a foot away from me. I thought I was a goner for sure."

"Me too." I took a deep breath and started toward the door. "We better get out of here."

Before we left the shop, we looked outside. In the autumn moonlight the parking lot was empty except for Evans's MG.

"Let's go," Parker said. Sticking to the shadows, we ran to the woods and raced through the underbrush, dodging tree trunks and stumbling over roots, barely noticing which direction we were going.

"Well," I said when we paused for breath. "What do we do now?"

"The police," Parker said. "We have to get the doll to the police."

I stared at him, not believing my eyes. In all the rush, I hadn't noticed he still had the doll. "Why didn't you leave it there?" I yelled at him. "Maybe they'd find it on the floor, think it fell out of the box or something, and forget about us."

Parker shook his head. "Flynn's not going to forget us or Pam either. You heard what he said this doll is worth."

"But Parker," I said, "if the cops get Evans and Flynn, they'll get Pam too."

"She'd be better off in jail than with either one of those crooks," he said. "God, Armentrout, what made her get involved in something like this? How could she be so stupid?"

I couldn't answer Parker, but I knew he was right about Pam. From what I'd seen of Flynn, I was sure she'd be safer with the police. A cold gust of wind knifed right through my jacket, and I shivered. "Let's get moving," I said. "If they've gone to my house, they'll be back this way any minute."

We ran on through the woods toward Blake Street, thinking we'd take the shortcut behind Jennifer's house, but just as we reached the edge of the woods, we heard Otis barking somewhere behind us.

"Quick!" Parker jumped Swenson's hedge, and I stumbled after him. We raced through their yard and the next three, dodging lawn furniture, bicycles, and woodpiles. Then we were scrambling over Jennifer's fence with Otis close behind, still barking happily as if he thought we were playing a wonderful game of hide-and-seek.

When we hit the ground, Jennifer's dog, a little poodle named King Tut, raced down the back porch steps, yapping and growling. Swerving away from his sharp teeth, I headed for the driveway but stopped when I saw a van, lights out, gliding silently down the street toward us.

Parker grabbed me and dragged me up Jennifer's back steps. He banged on the door till Jennifer lifted a corner of the shade and peeked out the window. In the meantime, King Tut had sunk his teeth in my leg, and Otis was prancing around Parker and me, his toenails clicking on the porch, his whole body wagging.

"Parker," Jennifer mouthed through the glass. "What are you doing here?"

"Let us in," Parker whispered. "It's an emergency."

Jennifer opened the door a crack. "I'm home alone baby-sitting," she said, "And Mom said I couldn't have anyone in the house."

Without another word, Parker pushed right past Jennifer, and we crowded through the door. Otis came too, and so did King Tut, still hanging on to my leg like a leech.

"Lock it!" Parker cried and helped Jennifer slide the deadbolt into place. Then he turned out the light and the three of us dropped to the floor, too scared to move.

"What's going on?" Jennifer whispered. She was staring at the doll.

"We're in big trouble," Parker said.

I had finally pried King Tut off my leg, mainly because he'd gotten interested in something else. He was staring at the kitchen door, growling deep in his throat, his body rigid. At the same moment, Otis forgot about the trashcan he'd been investigating and growled too.

The porch light was on, and I could see the shadow of a man looming up against the window in the door. Luckily the blind was down, so he couldn't see us crouching on the floor.

"Don't open the door, no matter what he says," Parker whispered.

Jennifer shook her head. I knew she wouldn't open that door for anything on earth.

"If Parker Pettengill is in there, please tell him his mother wants him." It was Evans, trying to sound just as nice and polite as he did when the old ladies with blue hair pulled up to his shop.

Jennifer whimpered a little, but she didn't say a word. King Tut and Otis, united by a shared danger, were still barking and growling, and I was making myself as small as possible.

"Parker," Evans said, "come on out. You and Matthew were supposed to be home by ten."

Evans's charming voice made it sound as if this were a simple case of a curfew violation, but no one was fooled. Otis hurled himself at the door so hard it shuddered, and King Tut leaped about hysterically. If only he'd been born a mastiff instead of a little poodle, I thought. With his disposition, he would have torn Evans into pieces and eaten him live.

The doorknob turned then, but the lock protected us. I looked at the window and imagined the glass breaking and Evans's hand coming in to open the door from the inside. And maybe that would have happened, if a car hadn't entered the driveway. As its headlights swept the kitchen, Jennifer whispered, "It's my parents."

At the same moment, we heard Evans run down the steps.

"What should we do?" I asked.

"Hide in the basement," Jennifer said, pushing us toward the stairs. "And keep that dog quiet."

Dragging Otis with us, we ran down the steps, through the recreation room, and into the laundry room. As the three of us crowded into a corner behind the dryer, we heard the back door open and the sound of parental voices asking if Tiffany had gone to bed on time and what was King Tut barking about? Had he upset the trashcan and made that mess all over the floor?

After answering their questions, we heard Jennifer tell her mother she wanted to see the rest of a movie she was watching in the basement. In a few seconds, she joined us in the laundry room.

Before we could explain what was going on, the doorbell chimed. Jennifer crept back up the stairs and peered out. "It's Mr. Evans," she whispered down to us.

As Parker grabbed Otis to keep him quiet, we heard Evans say, "Good evening, Mrs. Irwin. I'm looking for Parker Pettengill and Matthew Armentrout. Are they here?"

"Certainly not," Mr. Irwin said.

"Jennifer isn't allowed to have anyone in the house when we're out," Mrs. Irwin added.

"I'm sorry," Evans said, "but I'm sure I saw Jennifer let the boys in."

"You must be mistaken," Mr. Irwin said.

"Could I just talk to Jennifer then?" Evans persisted. "Parker's mother is so worried about him. He's been threatening to run away and she's just about at her wits' end. You can't imagine what she's gone through with that boy. The lies, the drugs, the sneaking around. . . ." Mr. Evans let his voice trail off suggestively as if there was more, much more he could say about Parker but decency forbade him to go on.

"I'm afraid we can't help," Mr. Irwin said, but at the same moment Mrs. Irwin called Jennifer.

Making a face, Jennifer left Parker and me in our corner, feeling helpless. All we could do now was hope Evans wouldn't trick Jennifer into giving us away.

# ·13·

AFTER FIVE MINUTES or so, Jennifer returned. "Is Evans gone?" I whispered.

Jennifer nodded. "He knows you're here, but my parents trust me too much to search the house like he suggested. Finally my father said he'd call the police if Mr. Evans didn't leave."

Suddenly Jennifer turned toward the stairs. "I think Mom's coming," she whispered. "Stay here and keep quiet."

As Jennifer ran into the recreation room, Parker and I crept back behind the dryer. Luckily Otis was sound asleep on a pile of dirty clothes, exhausted, no doubt, by the great hide-and-seek chase.

"Jennifer?" Mrs. Irwin's voice sounded too close for comfort. "Are you sure you haven't seen Parker and Matthew?"

"I'm positive," Jennifer said.

Her mother sighed. "I've always liked George Evans, but he made me very uncomfortable tonight. All that talk about Parker and Matthew getting into drugs. I just don't believe things like that happen in Woodcroft."

"Parker doesn't do drugs and neither does Matthew. Mr. Evans must be crazy or something," Jennifer said.

"He did act awfully strange," Mrs. Irwin said. "Why was he so sure the boys were here?"

"We went trick or treating earlier," Jennifer said. "Maybe Mr. Evans saw us walking home together and thought they came inside with me."

"I guess that explains it," Mrs. Irwin said, but she didn't sound totally convinced. Halfway up the stairs, she paused. "Be sure and go to bed as soon as the movie's over, Jennifer. We have a big day tomorrow."

Mrs. Irwin took a few more steps and stopped again. "Don't forget you promised to take Tiffany to the costume parade at eleven."

As soon as her mother was gone, Jennifer poked her head around the corner and beckoned us to join her in front of the television. Turning up the volume to drown out our voices, she looked at Parker and me expectantly.

"What's going on?" she asked.

Without answering her, Parker pulled a chair under one of the little basement windows and climbed up on it. Twitching back a corner of the curtain, he peered through the glass.

"Are they out there?" I whispered.

Parker shook his head. "I don't see the van." Then his back stiffened. "Evans is still there. He's standing in the shadows on the other side of the street." Jumping down from the chair, he slumped on the couch between Jennifer and me.

"Where do you think Flynn is?" I couldn't believe he'd go away. After all, he knew perfectly well where we were.

"He's taken Pam somewhere," Parker whispered.

"What are you talking about?" Jennifer asked. "Why is Evans after you?"

Parker and I looked at each other. "We have to tell her," I said. "She's in this with us now."

"What?" Jennifer leaned toward me, her eyes wide. "What am I in?"

"Lots of trouble," I said. "More trouble than you've ever been in in your whole entire life." I paused for a moment and tried to figure out a way to explain the situation we'd dragged poor Jennifer into.

While I was thinking, Parker took over. "It all started when we found the body," he said. "I saw Evans on the bridge that morning. We thought he killed the guy and dumped him in the creek, so we started watching the shop, trying to get proof. Tonight we found out what's going on."

He picked up the doll and showed it to Jennifer. "These things have hollow heads," he said. "Pam and Evans fill them with cocaine and then this other guy, Flynn, takes the dolls and sells them somewhere."

"A drug ring in Woodcroft? You must be kidding." Jennifer took the doll from Parker and stared at its sleeping face. "I don't believe you."

Impatiently, Parker grabbed the doll. Gripping its hair, he pulled the wig off and showed her the hole in the top of its head. Inside the cavity were two small bags of white powder.

We stared at each other, stunned by the sight of the cocaine. I could just see Flynn behind the counter of an antique store somewhere, selling the dolls to his customers. They wouldn't be little old ladies looking for dry sinks and settees and oak dressers. They wouldn't be mean guys on motorcycles looking for something to do in the woods, either. They'd be the kind of people you read about in news magazines—men in expensive suits, ladies in classy clothes.

"But why did Evans kill the guy you found in Indian Creek?" Jennifer whispered after a while. She was sitting close to Parker, her knees drawn tightly against her chest, her body tense.

"I don't think Evans killed him," Parker said. "He was just doing Flynn a favor. You know, dumping the body."

I cleared my throat, hoping to get a little of Jennifer's attention. "The dead man cheated Flynn," I said. "And now he thinks Pam and Evans are cheating him, too."

Parker swallowed hard and threw the doll across the room. It hit the wall and slid down in a heap of legs and arms. "I should've listened to you, Armentrout," he said. "None of this would've happened if I hadn't taken that damn thing."

"Don't worry about it now," I said. "Just figure out a way to get it to the police."

Without answering, Parker climbed back up on the chair and looked outside. "The van's back," he said. "It's parked half a block down the street."

"Let's call 911," Jennifer said. She jumped up as if she were about to run to the phone. "I bet the police would be here in five minutes."

"What's Flynn going to do if he sees a cop car pull up in front of your house?" Parker said. "Who knows where he's got Pam? He could kidnap her or kill her or anything."

"That's right," I said. "As long as Flynn doesn't think we've gone to the police, maybe he won't hurt Pam."

The three of us looked at each other. For once in his life, even Parker seemed stumped.

"I've got an idea," Jennifer said after a while. "I'm going to the costume parade with Tiffany tomorrow. Suppose I put the doll in her toy carriage? You know how crowded it gets during the Fall Festival. She could push her carriage right down Main Street to the police station. There'll be so many people, they couldn't possibly take the doll away from her. Even if they knew where it was."

Parker nodded hopefully, but I knew Tiffany a lot better than he did. She was just about as trustworthy as a baby copperhead. There was absolutely no telling what she'd do with the doll if she got her grubby little hands on it.

"I'll write a note explaining everything, and fasten it to the doll," Parker said. "When the cops find the cocaine they'll believe me."

Jennifer and Parker smiled at each other as if they'd solved everything, but I said, "What about us? How are we going to get out of here?"

"Oh, no," Jennifer said, "I didn't think about you two."

"Not to mention Otis," I said, as a snore from the laundry room reminded me of his presence.

"I've got it!" Jennifer cried. "Costumes! I'll fix you up so nobody will recognize you!"

While Parker and I watched, Jennifer ran to a closet and started pulling things out. She flung a slinky black dress at Parker and a pair of high heels. "You can be Vampira," she said. "I've got green makeup and a wig upstairs."

Then Jennifer tilted her head to one side and stared at me through narrowed eyes. Turning back to the closet, she rummaged around and tossed a bundle of gaudy clothes at me. "Here's my dad's old clown costume. With a few pillows stuffed in it, and makeup on your face, nobody will recognize you."

Parker held his dress up. "Are you sure this will fit?" he asked.

Jennifer nodded. "I'll pad the top," she said, "and make you look beautiful."

Parker laughed kind of nervously, but I could tell he was going along with the idea.

While Jennifer adjusted Parker's dress, I looked at the costume she'd given me. It was big and baggy and covered with garish polka dots. There was a curly multicolored wig to go with it. Unlike Parker, I was certainly not going to be eligible for any beauty prizes.

"But, Jennifer," I said. "What's your mother going to say when she sees us in the morning?"

Jennifer frowned and wrapped a long strand of hair around her little finger. She twisted it, thinking hard. Finally she grinned. "We'll get up early, and I'll pretend Parker's Linda Greene and you're Melissa Woltzman, and you came over to go to the festival with us."

"Melissa Woltzman?" I stared at Jennifer. "I hate Melissa. Why do I have to be her?"

"Well, Armentrout, you and Melissa have one thing in common," Parker said. "She's kind of plump." He poked my side and started laughing.

I glared at him. Here we were in a life-and-death situation and he was making fun of me. But before I could think of a good comeback, I heard Mrs. Irwin calling Jennifer.

"Isn't that movie over yet?" she yelled down the stairs in the sort of voice my mother uses when she's had just about enough of me.

"I'll be right up, Mom," Jennifer shouted. Turning to Parker and me, she said, "You can sleep on the couch. It pulls out into a bed. I'll come down early in the morning and help you with your costumes."

With Jennifer gone, the house seemed very quiet. Parker and I got the couch ready and found a blanket in the closet. Before he climbed into bed, Parker looked out the window again.

"The van's still there," he whispered.

"Do you see Flynn and Evans?" I asked.

"No. They must be inside." He crossed the room and lay down beside me. "Where do you think Pam is?"

"Maybe they let her go home," I said, realizing as I spoke they'd never do that.

"Flynn's got her somewhere," Parker said. "To keep her from going to the police."

"He won't hurt her," I whispered.

"I hope not." Parker's voice shook a little.

"He wouldn't *dare*." I tried to sound convincing, but I knew what Flynn had done to Dawson, and so did Parker. Now Flynn was suspicious of Pam and Evans. A lot of money was involved—thousands, maybe even millions of dollars. Flynn hadn't struck me as the sort of person who'd worry too much about killing anyone who got in his way, women and children included.

Upstairs a clock chimed twice. "We better go to sleep," I muttered. "Remember what Jennifer's mother said—tomorrow's a big day."

Parker sat up suddenly and stared down at me. "No

matter what happens, you're my best friend, Matthew. I want you to know that."

Although his hair hid his eyes, Parker's face was dead white in the moonlight, and I realized he was as scared as I was. My heart started going thunkety-thunkety like it does when I'm watching a horror movie. What had we gotten ourselves into?

"Nothing's going to happen," I said, "but if it does or it doesn't, you're my best friend, too."

Parker flopped back down. He didn't say anything else and neither did I. After a while, Otis climbed up and made himself comfortable between us. For once, I didn't mind if he breathed in my face. He was our protection, I thought, at least for now.

# ·14·

A T NINE THIRTY the next morning, Parker and I were sitting at the Irwins' kitchen table, trying to act like Linda and Melissa. So far, Mr. and Mrs. Irwin had been too busy getting ready for the festival to pay much attention to us. Obviously they were used to Jennifer's friends showing up at odd hours, and they weren't surprised to see us when they came downstairs.

Despite the green makeup and purple lipstick, Parker really did look beautiful. In his dress and long black wig, nobody would have suspected he was a boy. His only problem was his voice. To explain its huskiness, Jennifer kept asking him about his cold.

While everyone fussed over Parker, I slumped on a chair beside him. In a clown costume stuffed with two pillows, I felt fat and ridiculous. Jennifer had covered my face with white goop, stuck a round red ball on my nose, and topped me off with the rainbow-colored wig.

While she was transforming me, Jennifer and Parker had laughed themselves silly, but frankly I didn't see anything humorous about it. For one thing, the red ball hurt my nose and, for another, I wasn't allowed to eat because I might ruin my makeup. Then, of course, there was the van parked about a block down the street. With Flynn and Evans out there waiting for us, I couldn't even smile, let alone laugh out loud.

"I've never seen you girls so quiet," Mrs. Irwin said to Parker and me.

"Neither have I," Mr. Irwin agreed. "Usually it's giggle, giggle, giggle."

To my discomfort, I realized he was staring hard at me. "Your outfit reminds me of a costume I used to have," he said. Then, turning to Mrs. Irwin, he asked, "Whatever happened to my old clown suit? Maybe I could wear it today."

Without giving her mother a chance to answer, Jennifer dragged Parker out of his chair. "We're about ready to go," she said quickly.

Jennifer was disguised as a gangster. She'd borrowed an old pinstriped suit from her father and hidden her hair under one of his old hats. She was wearing fake glasses with a nose and mustache attached and carrying a water pistol made to look like a submachine gun. Like Parker and me, I was sure nobody would recognize Jennifer Irwin.

"Don't forget me." Tiffany, the little darling, my favorite kid next to Charity, strolled into the room pushing her doll carriage. I think she was supposed to be a mother, but in all honesty she looked more like a six-year-old Dolly Parton. She'd caked her face with blusher and bright red lipstick, poured mascara onto her eyelashes, and draped herself with so much costume jewelry she could hardly move. She was also wobbling about on her mother's high heels and wearing a satin dress with more padding than Parker had dared stuff into his Vampira gown. In a cloud of perfume, she stood there staring at us.

"What's Parker doing here?" she asked, looking right at him.

We all burst into loud and artificial laughter. "What are you talking about?" Jennifer asked. "Don't you know Linda when you see her?"

"Then what's Parker's dog doing in our backyard?" The adorable child pointed out the kitchen window.

Sure enough, there was Otis raising a leg to water the garbage cans. Jennifer had tied him up behind the garage, but he'd gotten loose and was now grinning at us and wagging his tail.

"Don't be silly. That's not Parker's dog," Jennifer said. "It's some other German Shepherd."

"Just get him out of the yard," Mr. Irwin said, "before he tramples the rosebushes."

We dashed outside and Parker grabbed Otis. "We can't be seen with him," he said. Hauling the dog behind the garage and out of sight, he managed to tie him up again. "Now stay, Otis. Stay!" he said firmly.

The dog whimpered and lunged after us, but Parker's knot held. Leaving Otis behind, we walked around the Irwins' house and joined Jennifer and Tiffany. Then we strolled toward Main Street, trying to look as casual as possible.

"Why are you wearing that dress?" Tiffany asked Parker. She was pushing her doll carriage along beside him, unaware of the antique doll hidden behind two smiling Cabbage Patch kids. "I know you're not Linda."

The three of us exchanged glances. Just ahead, parked on the corner, was the gray van. We hadn't fooled Tiffany, but maybe we'd fool Flynn and Evans.

"It's a game," Jennifer said. "Just pretend he's Linda, okay? If anyone asks, don't tell them he's Parker. We can win a prize at the Festival if we fool enough people."

"Will I get part of the prize?" Tiffany scowled at her sister. "I better or I'm telling."

"Yes, of course," Jennifer said.

Tiffany stopped and stared at Jennifer. We were right across the street from the van, but I didn't dare look at it.

"What's the prize?" she wanted to know.

"Candy," Jennifer said. "A big box. You can have it all."

Tiffany smiled then and pushed the carriage forward. "Look over there," she said to Jennifer. "Those men are wearing disguises, too."

That wasn't unusual. Almost everybody in Woodcroft dressed up for the Fall Festival. The mayor liked to call it our own little Mardi Gras.

Without turning my head, I glanced at the two men getting out of the van. Despite the rubber monster masks, I recognized Evans and Flynn.

"Just keep walking," Jennifer whispered to Parker and me. "There are lots of other people around. They can't do anything."

One block ahead was the Festival. I could smell Polish sausages and barbecue, I could hear the high school band warming up for the parade, I could see the senior citizens stirring the caldron of apple butter they made every year. Farther down the street were the craft stands, and I knew my mother must be there, selling her bread-dough ornaments and wondering where I was.

In between us and the Festival, though, were two men in monster masks.

"Tiffany," I said, leaning down to look her in the eye. "There's a part of the game we haven't told you yet."

She squinted at me. Her mascara was hanging from her eyelashes in big globs, and her teeth were coated with lipstick. "Matthew," she said. "I thought it was you!"

Out of the corner of my eye, I saw Flynn and Evans on the other side of the street, watching us. Maybe they didn't recognize Parker and me. Or maybe they were just waiting for a group of high school kids on skateboards to move on.

I shook my head and waggled my finger at her. "Remember, you don't know me or we won't win that prize."

Tiffany gave me what was no doubt supposed to be a conspiratorial wink which smudged her mascara. "So what am I supposed to do?"

"No matter what happens, even if somebody tries to stop you, you have to take your carriage to the police station and show them your dolls." I was sweating now. The sun was warm, and I was afraid my makeup was going to run.

Jennifer squeezed her sister's shoulder. "Scream if you have to," she said. "Just get those dolls to the police station."

"Will they give me the prize?" Tiffany asked. She was watching the skateboarders doing handstands as they rolled past us. Then her attention drifted to Evans and Flynn. "Why are those guys staring at us?"

"They're part of the game," Parker said. "They're the ones you mustn't talk to."

"And don't let them catch you," I said. "We'll all lose if they get you."

"This sounds like fun." Tiffany bared her little pointed teeth and grinned like a weasel. "I like games."

Then, swishing her hips, Tiffany started walking toward the Festival, pushing the doll carriage ahead of her. At the same moment, the skateboarders darted off like a flock of birds, leaving the street suddenly empty.

# ·15·

S TIFFANY DREW nearer to Evans and Flynn, she slowed down and looked back at us. We were standing there, the three of us, too scared to follow the poor kid.

When Flynn saw Tiffany hesitate, he crossed the street and blocked her path. "Hi, honey," he crooned through his monster mask. "Where are you going, looking so pretty?"

My heart sank. If Tiffany was anything like Charity, a little flattery would go a long way.

"To my grandma's house," Tiffany said, smiling sweetly. "And I'm not talking to any Big Bad Wolves."

Then, before Flynn knew what was happening, she kicked him sharply in the shins and started running toward the crowds on Main Street. The Cabbage Patch kids bounced up and down in the carriage. If they tumbled out, Flynn would see the doll hidden behind them.

But he'd already forgotten Tiffany. He and Evans were walking toward us.

"Okay, Parker," Evans was saying. "Fun and games are over now."

As Evans reached for Parker, Jennifer whipped out her machine gun. To my amazement, she pumped a spray of perfume into the eyeholes of his monster mask. Evans stumbled back, pawing at his face, and the three of us ran toward the safety of the Festival.

I saw Jennifer go one way, her long ponytail flying as her hat sailed off her head. Still clutching her machine gun, she was really moving. Although I wanted to stay near her, I thought I'd run to the right instead and make it harder for Evans and Flynn to round us up. As I turned the corner, I heard Otis barking and glanced back in surprise. How had the dog gotten loose?

Then I saw Flynn grab Parker. While they struggled, Otis hurled himself at Flynn, but the man kicked him aside and dragged Parker into the van.

For a second, I hesitated, wondering if I could help Parker. Then, realizing that Evans was gaining on me, I turned and ran into the crowd, pushing and shoving, using my elbows and feet, ignoring the yells and protests of the spectators. I thought if I put enough people between me and Evans, he wouldn't dare touch me. It was only a couple of blocks to the police station. Surely I could get there before he caught me.

But I hadn't figured on the principal of Letitia B. Arbuckle Junior High School. All of a sudden Mr. Arnold had me by the arm.

"Hold it right there," he bellowed just as if he'd caught me running in the hall at school.

All around me, people hemmed me in, trapped me. Like Mr. Arnold, they had been stepped on and pushed as I made my way through the crowd, and they were pleased to see me in trouble.

While I struggled to escape, I heard Evans excusing himself as he came toward me. He was still wearing his mask, but so were at least half the adults, including Mr. Arnold.

"I'm sorry, sir." Mr. Evans took my other arm and pulled me toward him. "My son and I were playing around and he got a little carried away."

"He's not my father!" I cried, but at that moment the drum and bugle corps drew abreast of us and every word I said was drowned out. As Mr. Evans dragged me off, no one thought it was any more than a case of a father disciplining his son.

Flynn was waiting a few feet away in the van, and Evans thrust me into the back beside Parker. He was already tied up, his wig crooked, his dress ripped, his makeup streaked. In a few second, I was tied up too, and the van was speeding out of town.

"Where's the doll?" Flynn asked. He'd taken off his monster mask, but I wished he'd kept it on. Believe me, he looked worse without it. His hair was sticking up in points, and he needed a shave. But it was the look in his eyes that scared me the most.

"Where's my mother?" Parker yelled.

"Let me take care of this," Evans said to Flynn. He climbed into the back of the van and grabbed Parker by the shoulders. "Quit fooling around," he said. "This is serious stuff, Parker. If that doll doesn't show up, we're in for it. You, Matthew, me, Pam, all of us!"

"Where's Pam?" Parker repeated. "What have you done to her?"

"I ask the questions around here," Flynn said. Yanking the steering wheel hard to the right, he turned the van onto a rough road.

Evans fell against me, cursing as he tried to regain his balance. Through the dusty windshield I saw nothing but the bare branches of trees, but I didn't need road signs to know where we were going.

While I was desperately trying to think of an escape plan, the van stopped. Just as I'd guessed, we were at the quarry, not far from Parker's and my fort. I could see the water through the trees.

"Okay, get them out," Flynn said.

Evans grabbed Parker and pulled him out of the van, then me. As Parker and I staggered around, trying to keep our balance with our hands tied behind us, I watched Flynn stride off through the woods toward our fort.

"Let him step in the trap," I prayed, "please let him step in the trap."

But he walked right past it, and I cursed myself for not helping Parker dig more holes. For a second, Flynn disappeared into our fort. Then he was coming back, still not anywhere near the trap, dragging Pam behind him. Her hair was tangled and full of leaves, her clothes were muddy and wrinkled, and she was tied and gagged. When she saw Parker, she tried to run toward him.

"Not so fast." Flynn grabbed her and pulled her back so hard she slammed against him.

"Don't hurt her," Evans said, starting toward Pam.

Pam was trying to talk, but the tape over her mouth muffled her words till Flynn yanked it off.

"Let Parker go," she sobbed. "For God's sake, he's only a kid. Please, please let him go!"

As Pam wept, I remembered how pretty she'd looked yesterday, driving off into the autumn sunset. It seemed as if a hundred years had passed since then.

When Evans moved toward Pam, she cried, "Leave me alone. You and your promises—I was a fool to help you."

"I didn't know it would turn out like this," Evans said. "If Parker hadn't been so nosy. . . ." He let the sentence trail off unfinished and glanced at Flynn.

"I'm really sorry," Evans told him. "It's just a little problem, nothing serious. I'm sure we can get it all sorted out and no harm done. Right?"

Flynn leaned against the side of the van and watched Evans through a haze of cigarette smoke. He didn't say anything.

"A couple of kids fooling around, making a nuisance of themselves, that's all," Evans went on. His voice shook and his forehead glistened with perspiration. "No big deal, old buddy."

Without looking at any of us, Flynn tossed his cigarette away and pulled a revolver out of his jacket pocket.

"No, Flynn, no," Evans cried out. "There must be another way. Make some threats, scare the hell out of them, then leave them here. By the time they get untied and walk back to town, you and I can be miles away."

He turned to Pam, talking faster now and louder, desperate to get Flynn's attention. "She won't talk, you can trust her." He reached out to stroke Pam's hair, but she ducked away from him. "Tell him, Pammy," he begged. "Promise him you won't go to the cops."

Flynn didn't look up from the gun. He was toying with it, making the cylinder spin. The woods were so quiet you could hear each tiny little click.

"He's right," Pam said. "Just leave us here. I'll make sure Parker and Matt keep their mouths shut."

"That's the way you see it," Flynn said to Evans. "We leave these three tied up in the woods, then you and me get in the van and drive off." He tossed the gun in a circle and caught it like a rodeo cowboy.

"Yes," Evans said eagerly. "That's it, Flynn."

When Flynn's eyes slid in my direction, I had a sudden vision of how I must look to him. A fat kid dressed in a clown suit, makeup streaked with tears and sweat, a rainbow-colored wig on my head.

"And how about you two?" Flynn asked, his eyes moving from me to Parker. "How do you see this little story ending?"

I bent my head and stared at the leaves covering the ground. In a few weeks, they would be brown and dry, but now they lay there in shades of yellow, red, orange, and deep purple. It had been a couple of years since I'd had an autumn leaf assignment, but I could still recognize the mitten shape of the sassafras, the points of the red maple, and the rounded curves of the oak.

A few feet away, a squirrel scurried about looking for acorns, and overhead a flock of crows flew by. Their loud caws broke the silence like shots.

"We won't say anything," Parker said.

"See?" Evans said eagerly. "Parker's a good kid and he's sorry for all the trouble he's caused." He smiled as if everything was settled. "Let's get out of here, Flynn."

Flynn watched Evans walk over to Pam, but he didn't move. He stayed where he was, leaning against the tree, the gun in his hand.

"I'm really sorry about this, honey," Evans said to Pam. "I hate leaving you here in the woods like this, and I don't blame you for being mad. But there's no other way, you can see that." He ran his hand gently down her hair, picking out the leaves, smoothing it back from her face while she stood motionless, looking at Parker, saying nothing.

"Please, Pam, tell me you understand," Evans said.

"Are you crazy?" Pam cried. Her hair lifted in a breeze and swirled around her face. At that moment, she was so beautiful it hurt to look at her. "If I get out of here alive, I never want to see you again!"

Maybe because Flynn was watching him, Evans frowned at her. "Hey, I was doing this for you," he said. "I don't remember you complaining about the new TV, the nice clothes, the fancy restaurants. You weren't worrying about Parker then, were you?"

Pam looked as if he'd slapped her. As she drew a deep breath, getting ready to say something, Flynn interrupted her.

"This has gone on long enough," he said. Raising the gun, he pointed it at Evans. "There's only one person leaving here today. Understand?"

Evans stumbled backward, shaking his head. "My God, John," he whispered, "what's one little slipup between friends? I'll make it up to you, pay you back somehow. There's no need to hurt anybody, no need."

"You knew the risks when you agreed to help me," Flynn said. His voice was flat and cold, his face expressionless. "You also knew what kind of man I am."

He glanced at all four of us, measuring us with his eyes as if he were deciding which one of us to shoot first. The woods were so quiet, I could hear my heart pounding as his eyes focused on Parker.

# ·16·

**P**OINTING THE GUN at Parker with one hand, Flynn grabbed him with the other. "For the last time, what did you do with that doll?"

Parker tried to pull away, but Flynn gripped him tighter and shoved the gun into his face. "Don't play with me, boy," he yelled. "You've pushed me far enough."

Letting go of Parker, Flynn punched him, sending him sprawling to the ground. As he stood over him, threatening him with the gun, I heard a crashing noise in the bushes behind us. Before Flynn had a chance to turn and confront him, Otis leapt at him, striking the man with the full force of his body. The gun flew out of Flynn's hand as he staggered under Otis's weight, and he fell on his face with the dog on top of him.

For a few seconds we stood still, too surprised to move. Then Evans must have realized he was the only one Flynn hadn't tied up. While Flynn struggled with Otis, Evans darted forward and grabbed the gun.

From the way his hands were shaking, I wasn't sure he knew what to do with it.

"Stay where you are," Evans said to Flynn. "Don't move!"

At that point, Flynn wasn't capable of getting up. He was too busy trying to keep Otis from tearing him to shreds.

With an eye on Flynn, Evans grabbed Pam. Ignoring her pleas to untie Parker and me, he forced her into the van. "They'll be okay," he told her as he started the engine. Then, while Pam struggled, Evans spun the van around and drove away.

Before they were out of sight, Flynn lurched toward us. His jacket was torn, his pants were ripped, he was bleeding. But, like a monster in a horror film, he was on his feet with Otis clinging to his arm.

Moving clumsily without my hands to balance me, I stumbled away from Flynn. Parker moved in the opposite direction toward our fort. Without hesitating, Flynn chose to follow him, not me.

With my back against a tree, I watched Parker dance away from Flynn almost as if they were playing a game of tag. Why wasn't he running faster? Then I realized what he was doing. Slowly and carefully, he was leading Flynn toward the trap.

Crazy as it sounds, Otis seemed to know what Parker was planning. He bit and growled and herded Flynn ahead of him as if the man were a sheep.

Then Parker stumbled and fell. Torn between running to his master and staying with Flynn, Otis hesitated. That gave Flynn a chance to break away from the dog and run forward.

Just as Parker planned, Flynn stepped on the branches and leaves covering the pit. They gave way with a loud crashing sound, and Flynn plunged into the hole.

"We got him, Armentrout," Parker yelled. "It worked!"

Fearfully, I joined Parker and peered over the edge. All I could see was Flynn's face two or three feet below and his hands, closer to the top but unable to get a grip on the muddy sides. The rest of him was wedged in the hole like a cork in a bottle. Without help, I was sure he couldn't get out.

Ignoring Flynn's threats and curses, we looked at each other. "We've got to get back to town," I said.

Parker nodded. His face was still tinged green from his Vampira makeup, except for a purple bruise below his eye.

As Otis jumped up to lick Parker's cheek, I noticed the piece of clothesline dangling from his collar. If the rope hadn't broken, Parker and I would be at the bottom of Bluestone Quarry right now. In spite of the warm sunlight, I shivered.

"Otis, you're the best and the smartest dog in the whole world," Parker said. Turning to me, he grinned. "Didn't I tell you he could track me down wherever I went?"

Another curse and more threats from Flynn erupted from the trap. "What should we do with him?" I asked Parker.

"Leave him here and get the cops," Parker said.

"What if he climbs out?" My heart sped up again as I imagined Flynn catching us before we reached the safety of town.

Parker led Otis to the edge of the trap. "Stay," he told the dog. "Don't let him out."

As we started to walk away, Otis whimpered. He watched us, his eyes pleading, but Parker shook his head. "Stay," he repeated firmly.

Obediently, Otis turned his attention to the hole. Crouching over Flynn, he growled horribly, and Parker said, "Good boy!"

It was hard to run with my hands tied, but I managed to stumble after Parker. We staggered through the woods to the road and started the long walk home.

Even though it was November first, the sun was still hot. I was hungry and thirsty and so tired my legs were shaking. Just when I was sure I couldn't take another step, I saw someone silhouetted at the top of the next hill. It was Jennifer running toward us.

"Thank God you're all right," she cried. "I saw Otis chasing the van, and I tried to follow him but I couldn't keep up."

"Are you okay?" Parker stared at Jennifer. Her face was dirty and streaked with tears, and her gangster suit was ripped in several places.

She looked down at herself and shrugged. "First I slid on some gravel and fell down," she said, "and then, when I was almost here, I saw the van coming really fast, and I jumped into the bushes to hide. Evans was driving like a maniac. I was sure you were dead."

I think Jennifer was about to hug Parker, but, before she could, he held out his hands. "Can you untie me?"

She pulled a Girl Scout knife out of her pocket and started sawing at the rope. "It's kind of dull," she apologized, but, in a couple of minutes, Parker's hands were free.

Then it was my turn. By the time Jennifer was finished, Parker was already at the top of the hill, running hard. Ignoring the stabbing pain in my side, I hurried after him.

# ·17·

WHEN WE WERE a block away from the police station, we saw Tiffany and Charity struggling to get the doll carriage up the steps and through the door. By the time we caught up with them, Charity was scowling at Sergeant Williams, and Tiffany was waving a Cabbage Patch Kid in his face.

"Parker said you'd give me a prize when I showed you my dolls!" Tiffany was saying.

"Where have you been all this time?" Jennifer yelled at her sister. "I told you to go straight to the police station!"

Tiffany looked at Charity. "She wanted to see the parade first," Tiffany whined, "and I was scared to come here all by myself, so I had to watch it, too."

Pushing Tiffany aside, Parker snatched the antique doll from the carriage and shoved it in front of Williams. "This doll," he gasped, still out of breath from running, "its head is full of cocaine!"

Tiffany and Charity stared at Parker. "How did that old thing get in my carriage?" Tiffany wanted to know.

"What's Parker doing in that dress?" Charity asked loudly. "He sure looks funny."

While Williams stared at him, probably wondering the same thing, Parker tried to explain about Pam and Evans and Flynn. "You've got to find my mother," he shouted, his voice cracking with desperation. "And arrest Flynn before he gets out of the trap and hurts my dog!"

"I saw the van on Endicott Road," Jennifer added. "It was going toward the Interstate."

"Look." Parker snatched the doll out of Williams's hands. Pulling the wig off, he dumped two little bags on the desk. "Cocaine!"

Williams shoved the bags toward our old friend Scruggs. "Have this checked," he said.

Then things started happening. Williams calmed us down somehow and got all the information we could give him about Flynn and what we thought was going on. Then he put out an all points bulletin for the van and sent a squad car to the quarry. Last of all, he sent somebody to Mom's and Mrs. Irwin's booths.

Before I even had a chance to decide what I was going to tell her, I saw Mom shove the door open and run toward me. Mrs. Irwin was right behind her. From the expression on Mom's face, I thought I was going to be killed after all. But I was wrong. Instead of yelling at me, she hugged me and started crying—

which was very embarrassing. Especially when you've just been a hero and trapped a dangerous drug dealer, and all the police are standing around watching your mother treat you like a baby.

As Mrs. Irwin left with Jennifer and Tiffany, Mom hugged Parker and Charity, though what my sister had done to deserve it I don't know. After all, it was her fault that Tiffany had taken so long to get to the police station.

Just when we were ready to go home, the squad car came back from the quarry. Flynn was slumped in the backseat, but Otis was riding up front beside the driver. His mouth was open and he was grinning like a hero. While Parker threw his arms around him, Otis winked at me, I swear he did.

You can make a bet Flynn didn't wink at anybody. In fact, he didn't even look up as the police led him past us. Besides being handcuffed and covered with mud, he was missing one shoe and the other was coated with clay from the bottom of the trap.

At the sight of his enemy, Otis growled. Hearing that, Flynn walked a little faster toward the door that led to the cells.

\*

When we got home, Mom fixed lunch for us, including a special treat for Otis, but Parker was too upset to eat. All he could think about was Pam. I was worried too, but I'm afraid that didn't stop me from devouring two tuna sandwiches and drinking three glasses of milk. We hadn't had anything to eat all day, and I didn't think my brain or my body could function much longer without some nourishment.

At last the phone rang, and Mom answered it. From what she was saying, Parker and I knew it was about Pam, and we listened hard, almost too scared to breathe.

When Mom hung up, she turned and put her arms around Parker. "George Evans wrecked the van," she said. "All he got were a few cuts and bruises, but Pam broke her leg. She's in surgery now, and you can see her tomorrow morning. I'll take you to the hospital."

She hurried us upstairs then, telling us we needed a bath and clean clothes and maybe a nap. You'd have thought we were five years old again, but the funny thing was, we did what she told us without a word of protest. In fact, my bed had never felt better in my whole life.

*

The next morning, Mom and I had a long argument. I thought she should take me to the hospital with Parker, and she thought I should go to school. If Parker himself hadn't begged Mom to let me come, I'm positive I would have found myself trudging down the street to Letitia B. Arbuckle Junior High School.

"Are you sure you want me to go in with you?" I asked Parker as we walked down the long gray hospital corridor. "Don't you want to be alone with Pam for a while?"

Parker shook his head. He was still very pale, and the bruise on his cheek had puffed up, making his eye almost disappear.

"Do you think she hates me?" he whispered.

"Why would she hate you?"

"It's my fault she's here, isn't it?" Parker slumped against the wall, his head down. "If I hadn't wanted to get something on Evans, none of this would've happened."

I had to lean toward him to hear what he was saying. "Are you kidding?" I asked. "You saw what kind of a man Flynn was. Sooner or later, Evans would've made a mistake, and he and Pam would have ended up like the dead man in Indian Creek. You probably saved her life, Parker."

He shrugged and ran a hand through his hair, pushing it straight back from his face. Of course, it tumbled down in his eyes again.

"Come on," I said, even though I was kind of scared to see Pam myself. "Let's go in."

When Parker didn't move, I took his arm and steered him past the policeman sitting in a folding chair beside the door.

Pam was lying in a bed with sides like a crib, and an IV was attached to her arm. Her leg was in a cast up to her hip and her head was bandaged. She was so still, I was scared she was dead.

The rubber soles on Parker's shoes made a loud squeaking sound on the tile floor, and Pam opened her eyes. To my relief, she smiled. "Parker," she whispered, "thank God, you're all right. They told me you were safe, but I was afraid to believe them."

While I stood there watching, Parker dropped to his knees beside the bed. "I'm sorry," he sobbed. "I never wanted you to get hurt."

"It's all my fault," Pam said. With her free hand, she reached out and brushed Parker's hair out of his eyes. "How can you ever forgive me? If it hadn't been for Otis, we'd all be dead."

When Pam started to cry, I knew I should leave, but they'd forgotten all about me. I didn't want to embarrass them by trying to tiptoe out the door.

"But, why, Pam?" Parker asked. "Why did you do it?"

She wiped her eyes with the back of her hand. "Oh, Parker," she sniffed, "I was so stupid. George made it sound like such an easy way to get some extra money. There were things I needed for the house, for you, for me, so I started helping him with the dolls. Then, I don't know, I thought I loved him, I thought he'd marry me, take care of us, make life easier."

She turned to Parker and her voice rose a little. "You don't know how hard it's been all these years, trying to raise you all by myself. No extra money, hardly enough to pay the rent and buy the groceries. I know it was wrong, but I never thought anyone would be hurt."

Reaching up, she gently touched Parker's bruised cheek. "I'm sorry," she whispered. "If I ever get out of jail, I'll be a better mother, honest I will."

"Jail?" Parker drew back and started at Pam, stunned. "They won't put you in jail, will they?"

"What do you think happens to people who sell drugs?" Pam turned her face away. "The police don't just pat you on the head and tell you not to do it again," she whispered.

Before Parker could say anything more, a nurse appeared with a cartful of little tubes. Stepping up to the bed, she put her hand on Parker's shoulder.

"That's enough for now," she said. "Your mother needs to rest."

Parker rose slowly to his feet, and the nurse smiled at him. "You can come back tomorrow," she added kindly.

Stealing one last look at Pam's pale face, I followed Parker out of the room. I could see how upset he was, and I wished I could think of something comforting to say. But what can you tell your best friend when his mother is going to jail? As far as I know, even Dear Abby hasn't got any advice about a subject like that.

*

That afternoon, Parker and I were sitting on my back steps. He had been unusually quiet ever since we left the hospital, and I wondered what he was thinking about.

After a long stretch of silence, Parker looked at me. Mom had trimmed his hair, and I could actually see his eyes.

"What do you think will happen to Pam?" He pulled Otis close and gave him a hug.

"Dad's going to talk to a lawyer," I said. "He thinks if Pam gives evidence against Evans and Flynn, the judge might go easy on her."

"Will they put her in jail?"

"I don't know," I said. "But whatever happens, my mom says you're staying with us. You and Otis both."

"Really?" Parker smiled for the first time all day. "I was afraid they'd put me in a foster home or something." He buried his face in Otis's fur and hugged him hard.

At that moment, Jennifer came around the corner of the house. Tiffany and Charity were right behind her but they were too involved in one of their games to pay us any attention.

As Jennifer sat down between Parker and me, I heard Tiffany yell, "Quick, run, Flynn's coming. He'll kill us, he'll kill us!"

Charity gave an ear-piercing scream, and she and Tiffany tore past us as if they were truly being chased.

"Help, Help!" they cried. "Save us, Otis, save us!"

Otis sat up straighter and watched them disappear behind the garage. Then he turned to Parker and said, "Whuf?"

"So now it's just a kids' game," Parker observed.

"Not to me." Jennifer shivered. "Not ever."

"Me either." I slid nearer to Jennifer, wishing she weren't sitting so close to Parker.

Otis got to his feet and gave himself a little shake. Then he ambled off toward the garage to check on Tiffany and Charity.

"Maybe he wants to be a hero again," Parker said.

The three of us looked at each other and smiled. I think we'd all had enough heroism for a while.

Behind us, I heard Mom in the kitchen getting dinner ready, and I knew Dad would be home soon. At five thirty on the dot, we'd sit down at the table, and Charity would complain about something on her plate, and Dad would threaten to send her to her room. After dessert, Parker and I would go up to my room and work on this month's book report.

For once in my life, I was perfectly content. The fragrance of an apple pie baking in the oven tickled my nose, and the November sunlight was still warm enough to feel good on my face. At that moment, I didn't care if anything exciting happened to me again for a long, long time.

# SEARCHING FOR A GOOD MYSTERY?
# CHECK OUT THESE TALES OF SUSPENSE!

**Double Trouble Squared**

**Shadows in the Water**

**A Voice in the Wind**

**The Starbucks Twins Mysteries** by Kathryn Lasky

Meet sleuthing telepathic twins in this trio of exciting tales by the author of the best-selling Guardians of Ga'hoole series!

## The House on Hound Hill
by Maggie Prince

"Fascinating and eye-opening . . . will satisfy fans of fantasy, mystery, and historical fiction."—*SLJ*

## A Murder for Her Majesty
by Beth Hilgartner

★ "The suspense in Hilgartner's gripping mystery is balanced by the fascinating details of daily life at the York Minister during the Elizabethan era." —*SLJ*, starred review

## There's a Dead Person Following My Sister Around by Vivian Vande Velde

"A fast-paced story that mixes scares and history for some can't-put-it-down fun." —*Kirkus Reviews*

## Sweet Miss Honeywell's Revenge
by Kathryn Reiss

"An enjoyably sinister read." —*The Bulletin*

## Mystery in Mt. Mole
by Richard W. Jennings

★ "Outrageously imaginative . . . readers are treated to lots of tongue-in-cheek humor." —*Booklist*, starred review